UNWRAPPED #for you

A CURVES FOR CHRISTMAS NOVELLA

I0747540

ANNIE CHARME

CHAMBRE ROSE PUBLISHING

This is a work of fiction. Names, characters, organisations, places, events, and incidents are either products of the author's imagination or are used fictitiously.

First Published in 2022 by Chambre Rose Publishing

Unwrapped For You. A Curves For Christmas Novella

First Edition

Print ISBN: 978-1-7399906-4-0

Formatted by: Chambre Rose Publishing

 Created with Vellum

Happy Holidays to all my readers.
May your bed be warm and your stocking full.

This book is written by a British author. Therefore all spellings and grammar are British English.

And yes, we call our cats 'pussycats' here

Contains:
Mature themes and graphic content
some fat-phobic remarks from a colleague.
Discussions on a family member battling with multiple sclerosis.

Part of the Curves for Christmas Collaboration

One

EVE

A thousand miles from home, my heart yearns for the blustery autumn wind and rain back in the UK. I inhale the fresh November air, catching the scent of cedar from the trees. A ball darts past me, and I turn my head, eyeing thick rugby thighs running beside a golden retriever. I shouldn't stare, but the Lycra and muscle have me in a trance, not to mention the black inked pattern on his chest and washboard abs.

His dog picks up speed, veering off, and heads in my direction, bounding over almost in slow motion with his tongue lolling out. I look around to see what caught the dog's attention; the ball maybe?

A thump to my chest, then my legs fail me as I tumble backwards onto the soft grass. My bum is the first thing to hit the ground, taking most of the blow. It's a good thing I have plenty of padding in that region.

Turns out, the dog had his eye on me, and now his

tongue. He's a dominant force, pinning me beneath him while licking my face. I wonder if his owner is this forceful. Oh, he's here.

"Diesel. Diesel. Down, boy." He whistles, but Diesel fixates on licking my face.

I can't stop the giggle that pours out of me, and I give Diesel a good ruffle behind his golden ears. "Hello Diesel, nice to meet you too."

His rough tongue wets my neck, then he nuzzles down the valley of my breasts, over my buttoned dress, down to my stomach, and another giggle escapes as his nose tickles my belly.

"Diesel." His owner's voice is gruff, but the dog still isn't taking any notice. He stands over me and tries to pull the dog from me, but Diesel nuzzles into my squishy stomach, tickling me more. "I'm so sorry, miss. I don't know what's got into him."

"Oh, it's okay." I ruffle his fur again. "You can smell my pussy, can't you, Diesel?"

Hot thigh guy's brown eyes widen, and I realise what I said, crossing my legs to prevent Diesel from sniffing there.

Heat claws at my neck. "Er. He can smell my kitty. I mean my cat. My pussy...cat. I have a ginger pussy. Oh, gosh." My hands cover my face to hide the flush in my cheeks.

Diesel's still going to town, his wet nose trailing up and down my legs like a slug on speed, threatening to dive under my dress at any minute.

I hear a chuckle.

"When the earth has swallowed me whole, let me know so I can open my eyes."

He chuckles again, this time getting a good grip on Diesel's collar, lifting him from me, but the dog dives back down, trying to nuzzle between my legs.

"Damn, he really likes the smell of your pussy...cat."

I open my eyes and tug my dress back down to my knees to hide my dimply thighs.

He coughs and clears his throat. "I'm Liam." He holds out a hand to pull me up.

Once on my feet, I brush the dirt and grass from my clothes. "I'm Eve."

"I'm sorry about my dog. I don't know what got into him."

"I do."

"Yeah, your pussy. Perhaps I should see what all the fuss is about." He raises an eyebrow.

"She's cute and fluffy."

"Like her owner?" His biceps bulge as he strains to keep Diesel under control and prevent him from going in for the kill on my crotch.

Just looking at the dog's slobbering jaw is enough to make me keep my legs crossed. That's the last time I'm stepping out after having Jingles on my lap. Or maybe that little wildling has done me a favour. I bat my lashes at Liam and give him my widest smile. The heat from my cheeks must glow, but he's hot, too. Hotter than the Texas sun in a heatwave.

He moves his hand through his dark hair, pulling it back from his face. It flops back down over his forehead in a messy, ruffled, but hot-as-hell way that makes me want to run my fingers through it.

"Do you want to get a coffee? I'll take Diesel home.

He's not invited after his behaviour. I can promise I'm much more of a gentleman."

"Now I'm disappointed." I bite my lip, twirling a lock of hair, my best attempt at flirting.

He laughs. "Well, only on first encounters."

"I'd love to get a coffee. I don't know many people here."

"I thought I detected a British accent." His grip tightens on Diesel's collar as he attaches the lead.

"I moved here just over a week ago for work." I relax when Liam secures the lead on Diesel, knowing the dog won't be nuzzling under my dress again, but then a gust of wind blows through my curls and wafts the fabric around my legs.

He glances toward the heavens. "Looks like rain anyway. We should head back before we get drenched."

I pull my jacket over my dress to block out the wind and Liam unwraps a hoody from around his waist and pulls it over his head, covering his ribbed stomach that I was getting accustomed to.

"Damn weather reporters. They said it was going to be dry today."

I snap my head to the side. "You can't blame the reporters."

"Why? They always get it wrong. Couldn't predict rain during a monsoon."

"I think that's a little unfair. They only report on the data given. They're not psychic."

He huffs. "The data? What data? They go outside, wet their finger and hold it up in the air." He gives a chuckle at his own—not funny—joke.

My fists dig into my hips. "Meteorology is actually a complex science that requires a four-year degree."

"What a crock of shit."

I pinch my eyebrows together at his insolence. My body temperature rising as my pulse quickens with fury. "It's true."

"Why are you getting all huffy? It's not like you're a meteorologist." He chuckles. Then stops when he sees I'm not laughing, giving him a death stare. "Are you? Shit, I didn't think—"

"Why, because I'm a woman?" The blood in my veins reaches boiling point, my face burning as hot as the sun.

"No, I—"

"Save it." My head may explode if he carries on speaking. I've dealt with plenty of male chauvinists over the years. I certainly don't need to take this from a poser and his randy dog. Even if he caused a flood in my knickers with his shirt off.

I shake my head to get the visions of his bare chest and ink out of my head, turn around and storm off against the gaining wind.

"I never meant that. Where are you going?" he shouts after me.

I keep walking, but not before spinning on my heel. "I'm going to wet my finger and stick it in the air. Gotta get tomorrow's report."

Making a swift escape, I leave him in the park with Diesel. Did I overreact? Nope. He's just like all the other self-centred pricks I've met; hence why I'm here, in Texas. I studied for years, analysing the data. I should be able to report it too. Back in the UK, I was always behind the scenes. Each time a position arose for a weather broadcaster, I was pushed aside in favour of a pretty girl.

The final straw was to find out that the uneducated girl —with a pinched waistline and legs for days—who rocked up in time for hair and makeup and read out my report, was earning more money than me.

I pull out my gold keycard to my new apartment at Fitzpatrick Place just as the rain starts. Holding my jacket over my head, I dart through the courtyard. Uncle Graham's place costs more than I would usually pay for an apartment, but I fell in love with the quaint, gated two-story complex. The pool was a bonus.

Jingles greets me as I open the door to my ground floor apartment in the two-story complex. She rubs against my leg with a meow, then scampers like something spooked her. She must have smelt that dirty dog on me. Although, I think I prefer the dog to its owner.

Two

LIAM

Back at my apartment, a posted letter lies on my floor. Diesel runs through the room to the sliding patio doors at the back, barking at the neighbour's tormenting cat. He scratches against the glass, whining to get out, but I'm not falling for that again. Yesterday was carnage.

I open the letter. The new resident next door is blaming Diesel for smashing her precious plant pots, which aren't even hers. The previous tenant left them.

Kicking off my running shoes, I read it again with anger bubbling in my veins.

Dear sir,
I was horrified to come home yesterday
to find broken pots all over my patio. A

resident informed me your dog was on a rampage.

What's even more disheartening is that you haven't shown me the common decency of an apology.

I demand that you replace my pots and clean up my patio at your earliest convenience. In the meantime, a sorry or acknowledgement to my letter would be appreciated, seeing as I can never catch you home.

Your neighbour at apartment A8

I huff. Neighbour? Crazy cat lady is what she is. I haven't met her yet, but she sounds like a stuck-up snob. And if she thinks she's blaming my dog for her demented cat's actions, she has another think coming.

Tossing the letter on the hall table, I walk into the bedroom, needing a shower. Diesel's still barking through the window at that damn cat. "Here, boy."

He bounds in, fussing around my leg with his tail wagging for some attention.

"Good boy." I close the curtains to take away the temptation. I've never been a fan of pussies unless we're taking about the soft kind that don't bite.

My mind wanders to the girl at the park as I step into the shower, the warm water hitting my face, taking away the November chill. I wouldn't normally pick up a girl at the park, but there was something about her lying flat out on her back looking vulnerable while Diesel licked up her thick thigh and damn, I wished it was me.

I shake the water from my hair as if shaking her from my mind. The chances of seeing her again are slim in this bustling city, not to mention how I pissed her off. Why couldn't I keep my mouth shut? When she said she was a meteorologist, I knew I'd fucked up.

It wasn't that I assumed she wasn't a meteorologist because she was a woman at all. I've just never met one before. I didn't go to college. Barely made it through high school. An intelligent woman is attractive. Unfortunately, they're out of my league. When it comes to wanting a deep intellectual conversation, I mask my IQ by making jokes.

A silent laugh rocks through me, picturing her sassy ass swaying as she walked away, and I almost want to see her again just to tease and annoy her.

Three

EVE

Ugh. The hellhound next door just won't stop barking. What is it with me and dogs since I moved here? Poor Jingles is terrified of going outside and has been climbing the walls since we moved in. I need to say something.

With her nocturnal habits, I've always left a small window open that acts as a cat flap. It's never been an issue in the UK, but here, each time she goes out to do her business, the mutt starts. I can't carry on like this. I'm up at 4 a.m. for work. It's not all sunshine and rainbows getting up at that time.

The clock strikes midnight. I should be in the land of nod, but in my rage I'm throwing on a dressing gown and marching to my neighbour's door. A light shines through the window. Claws on wood scratch from one room to the other as I knock.

A man's voice says, "All right, all right. Calm down, D. It's just the door."

Just the door? I'm like a whirlwind. He won't know what hit him.

The hinge creaks as the door opens. My jaw drops. Hot thigh guy, I mean rude thigh guy, stares at me with a gaping mouth, making me wish I'd dressed better. My hand smoothes over my messy hair, and I pull the dressing gown closed over my body.

My eyes glide over his inked chest down to his black boxers, hugging his package and wrapping tight around those muscly thighs.

He clears his throat. "Eve? How the hell did you find me?"

My brow furrows. "I'm not stalking you, if that's what you think." Who does he think he is? Like I would have looked him up, then called round in my nightclothes. For what? A quickie? Another ploughing from his dog? No, thank you.

Bugger my baubles, think of the devil, and he will appear. Diesel knocks Liam to the side and goes right for me, nuzzling inside my dressing gown, exposing my little satin short set that barely covers my large breasts and even larger thighs.

"Diesel. No." Liam grabs his collar, tearing him away from me, but not before he gets a good look at my ensemble. "I'm sorry, come in. Are you all right? Can I call someone? You can stay here if you need to." He wrestles with Diesel, keeping him close.

"I'm not homeless. I live next door, you plonker." I fold

my arms over my chest in a huff. Even the sight of his fine body isn't enough to soften me when I'm tired.

"Plonker?"

I roll my eyes. "Please stop your dog from terrorising my pussy...cat. I have to be at work in four hours."

"That ginger fluff ball is yours?"

"Yes. I told you I had a ginger fluff...ball. Pussy. Cat. Ugh." Why can I never speak properly with him? My gaze floats down again to those beefy legs. *Snap out of it.*

"Well, I suggest you keep that pussy of yours locked up. She parades up and down my patio like some hooker, flaunting it just to torment my dog."

"How dare you? It was your dog that came onto my patio and broke all my pots, which you still owe me for, by the way."

"That note was from you?" He shuts the door in my face.

Every muscle in my body tenses for all the wrong reasons. I lift my hand to knock again, but the door flies open.

He holds my letter in his hand. "This is what you can do with your note." He crumples it into a ball in his tight fist. "I won't be replacing any of your plant pots when your ginger floozy is the one to blame."

My eyes widen. "We'll see about that." I shake my head and turn around as he pulls his big golden retriever inside. He's still barking. Is it me or my kitty he wants?

I march off in my fluffy slippers that are cushioned underfoot, which doesn't give me the stomping effect I want, but the slamming of my door should be enough of a signal for him to know I'm pissed.

I lock the small kitchen window that acts as a cat flap. "Sorry Jingles, you'll have to use the litter tray tonight, girl."

Ugh. Why are all the good-looking guys complete arseholes? I had my doubts when I met him in the park. Now he's confirmed it. My last neighbour back in England was a complete twat, too. For too long, I put up with his rudeness. Well, not anymore. I'm tired of being a pushover.

Four

EVE

My eyes are still bleary as I slump into Bourbon's TV studio, a large, tall building with mirrored glass that glistens under the streetlights. The morning chill at this ungodly hour has me pulling my jacket closed over my chest as I head straight to the canteen for my morning coffee.

"Morning, Eve. Are you all settled into your new place?" My uncle Graham says with a British twang. He's lived in Texas for years, but still has a hint of our Yorkshire roots.

I glare at him. No wonder he was so quick to give up his apartment for me. "Yeah, I'm loving the neighbour and his dirty dog. I'm not sure which one of them is the most annoying, Diesel or his owner."

My uncle Graham comes to a halt and spins around. "You met Liam?"

I roll my eyes. "It's hard not to when his dog won't leave me alone."

He scratches his beard. "They never gave me any trouble when I lived there. Is he hounding you?"

I huff into my cup of coffee. "You could say that."

"Stay away from Liam. He's all right, but don't get involved with someone like him. It's not good for your wholesome weather girl image."

I squish my eyebrows together. Surely with those pectorals and muscular thighs he would do my image good. Unless he has some shady past.

"Catch up with you later. Are you coming over for dinner? Jay's cooking." Graham turns around and rushes off as quickly as he came, making his way to the graphics studio with a bundle of sports reports in his arms.

"Sure," I holler after him as I stroll to the daily conference with the team.

Being a weather girl isn't as glamorous as it appears. Anyone who saw me before hair and makeup would vouch for that. I stare at the synopsis, trying not to yawn while taking notes about the local temperatures. It's all technical jargon that I need to present in layman's terms so people will know whether to wear a coat or grab their umbrella before leaving the house.

An image of Liam pops into my head. The part where he wet his finger to see which way the wind was blowing. I can't help but smile at how silly that statement was. What a tool.

After eyeing the graphics templates, it's time to be beautified. Lisa, our resident stylist, truly is an artist. I scarf down a bagel and another coffee while she runs her fingers and a hot iron through my curls, then pull out my phone. What did Graham mean when he said my neighbour wasn't good for my image? I wonder what his last name is. Bourbon City News is a reputable station that prides itself on being a wholesome family firm.

Tapping my manicured nails against the dressing table while Lisa dusts me in a fine powder, I wonder if Fitzy would know his name. She seems to know everything that goes on in those apartments. *Why don't you just ask him?* Ugh. I don't want Liam to know I'm stalking him. He already thought I'd fled last night, rocking up at his home like some damsel in distress.

Before going live on air, I smooth my palms down my fitted blue dress. It's a little tighter than it was the last time I wore it.

"Eve, don't you have something more flattering? The camera adds ten pounds," Dirk, the cameraman says. Talk about giving me a boost of confidence before I go on air. The girls don't call him Dirk the Jerk for nothing.

"A good cameraman knows how to get the best angles." I stick my chin out, getting into position.

At least Lisa has made me look alive and not the withering corpse I was at 4:30 this morning. I've had little to no sleep thanks to my excessively hot, but apparently unsavoury neighbour, which now has me even more intrigued at what he's hiding. *He wasn't hiding much last night,* my subconscious says, making me smile inwardly.

"Action," Dirk says, panning the camera to me.

I give my brightest smile and read my report from the teleprompter. "After a long dry spell." *Not kidding.* I can't remember the last time I had a man. "We're finally seeing some precipitation." *Perspiration more like.* Is it hot in here? I can't get visions of Liam's hunky body out of my mind.

"Moist bodies." I shake my head. "I mean moist air mixed with low pressure, creating bodies of water."

Dirk squishes his caterpillar eyebrows at me. I'm waffling. He gives me the nod to wrap this show up.

"So as we start the countdown for Christmas and the weather is getting wetter, make sure you have your brolly. Baby, it's getting cold outside." I give a sheepish smile and a little wave as Dirk cuts and the studio goes to a commercial break.

"What was that?" Molly, from the sound crew says.

Heat claws at my neck. "I'm just tired. Was it that bad?"

"Just a bit weird. I'm sure no one noticed, but what the heck is a brolly?"

I cover my mouth with my hand, realising people here aren't familiar with my Yorkshire lingo. "An umbrella."

"Oh." She waves a hand. "Anyway, are we still on for drinks at the weekend?"

"Sure."

She swishes her hair and walks off as the crew set up for the morning news.

This cannot happen again. That pain in my neck isn't gonna ruin my career. I've worked too hard to get this position.

"Eve, great report. That last line was perfect. The public has really warmed to you." My boss pats my arm, his ultrabright teeth almost blinding me under the studio lighting, along with his salt-and-peppered hair highlighted by the fluorescents.

"Really?" I flinch my head back in surprise, the heat still creeping up to my cheeks from the sheer embarrassment of fumbling my words on set.

My uncle appears. "You're trending on our website. Bourbon's new force to be reckoned with, one follower commented."

No prizes for guessing who that could be.

Graham slides his index finger over his phone. "English beauty, weather girl, Eve Snow, melts Bourbon's Texan hearts with her genuine, down-to-earth demeanour and British humour."

So they like it when I cock up? Liam may have done me a favour.

"It's nice to see an everyday girl next door on our TV." Graham continues to read off the comments in front of the boss, Stan. He's basically just blowing smoke up my arse, so I let him continue while I'm on a roll.

"Very good. Keep up the great work, Eve." Stan blinds me one last time as he smiles and walks away. "Oh, as an employee you get free gym membership at Fit & Flex." He waves a hand, then continues to walk out of the studio.

"Was that a dig at my weight?"

Graham rolls his eyes. "Eve, not everything is a dig at your weight."

"Stan isn't the first today. Dirk basically said I need to lose weight. *The camera adds ten pounds*," I mock in Dirk's voice. "I know this dress is a little snug, but I don't see how that's anybody's business."

Graham places a large paw on my shoulder. He's a burly man, like a grizzly bear. If anyone can understand my plight, it's him. "Why do you always react?"

I blow out a huff of air. "I don't know. Years of being bullied for being overweight, maybe." My eyes swell at the memories.

He pulls me into a bear hug, his beard scratching my cheek. "I get it, but look at this as a fresh start. You can't live in the past."

I rub at my temple. "I know you're right. But you're a bloke. You have no idea what it's like being a woman who's worked her arse off in a man's world, where I'm the odd one out." Most men don't value intelligence over looks. It's why I always think the worst. It's something I need to work on, but when I'm surrounded by jerks like Dirk, it's hard to weed out the guys who are genuine.

"Try being a gay bloke in a man's world." His lips quirk in the corner.

"Fair enough." A smile pushes my cheeks up.

"Stan just wanted you to know about the gym subscription. All the guys here are big into their fitness, that's all."

My eyes widen. "Does this mean he expects to see me there?"

"Just show your face once a week."

"Once a week? Are you having a laugh? I didn't know that was part of the job description." If they think I'm going to lose weight to fit in with societal norms, they have another think coming. "As if keeping up a wholesome TV persona isn't enough."

Uncle Graham chuckles to himself. "Eve, you have no problem with keeping your wholesome persona. Let's face it. You're not exactly a party animal."

Graham didn't need to spell it out for me. He thinks I have a boring life.

"I can party. It's just I don't have anyone to party with." In my frustration, I spin around and storm off to the canteen in need of chocolate.

After years of fad diets, I've finally learned to love my body. I'm proud to showcase my figure on screen. It's about time we had more plus-size representation and diversity in the media.

Five

LIAM

Rubbing my eyes, I make a smoothie and turn on the TV in the kitchen. I rub my eyes again when I see a vision in blue presenting the weather. It's like a cold front appearing out of nowhere. I chuckle to myself, watching her talk about low pressure, and a wave of heat comes over me. She looks pissed, like she did last night.

A smile creeps over my face. I never thought I'd see her again after our minor altercation in the park. It's clear why Diesel's been barking nonstop this last week. If I'd known she was next door, I'd be scratching the door down to get to her, too. Damn, she looked good in that satin short set. If only she wasn't so uptight.

She should join the gym. She could work off her anger issues. Or better still, I could give her a workout of my own, but first, she needs to be brought down from the clouds. Miss Meteorologist High and Mighty, me and my pussy are too good for you.

Diesel sits on the kitchen tiles, staring up at me, waiting for his breakfast. I ruffle his ears, thinking about how I can get her to lighten up. We are neighbours after all. "Dude, we gotta work together on this. You gotta have my back. No more hounding her pussycat."

Diesel tilts his head to the side and whines with big eyes.

"You leave her pussy to me, you hear?" I pour his kibble into a bowl, then watch Eve getting all flustered on screen, talking about being moist. Another chuckle rumbles in my chest as I fill Diesel's water bowl. My morning routine just got better.

In my mind, I'm already conjuring up all the ways I can tease her while my fingers tap the screen on my phone, loading the news website. A smile curves my lips when I type in the comments section: Bourbon's new force to be reckoned with.

I set my phone up to record myself on the bench and almost drop the weight when I spot Eve saunter into the gym in a pair of tight yoga pants clinging to her thighs. A baggy t-shirt covers her ass, but lying down from this angle gives me the vantage point to see her round cheeks peeking out from the bottom of her top.

I sit up as she approaches and wipe the sweat from my brow. "Hey, weather girl."

She stops in her tracks, gripping her water bottle. "Ugh, not you again."

I stand in front of her with a grin plastered on my face. "Still frosty?"

Her eyes roam my chest. "Don't you own a shirt?"

"Well, you seem to like me topless." I grab the phone and stop the recording, knowing I have her recorded with her heated stare. Even if she is trying to give off an icy glare.

She walks past me towards the treadmills, reluctantly stepping onto a free one, then sets it, going at a snail's pace.

The one beside her becomes free, and I jump on before it's taken again. "What's got you in a mood today?"

She pinches her eyebrows together as she stares at me, still trudging on the treadmill. "I wonder? Could it be the hound that howls all night, keeping me up for the last week?"

"I'm sorry. He's not normally like this. He has a thing for ginger fluff balls. Who knew?" I can't stop the grin from forming, but she isn't amused. "We should get together. You know, once he's played with your pussy, he might lose interest."

"Ugh, like a typical man, then? Is that what you do?" She's out of breath, doing a slow walk at a steady incline. Or is it me that's getting her all flustered?

"I'm not that sort of guy." It's tiring being stereotyped all the time. Just because I like to work out and hang at the gym, people assume I'm a player. "Truth is, I used to be a scrawny weed back in school. One day I was tired of the bullies, so I learned to fight back. Mom sent me to the local gym for boxing lessons, and it became my sanctuary."

She studies me for a moment, chewing on the inside of her cheek. Her eyes sadden as if she sympathises. "I hope you gave the bullies what they deserved."

"They got what was coming to them." A smile curves my lips thinking of my revenge. I was never good at academic stuff, but I found something I enjoyed that I was good at and it's served me well so far.

She pulls out a Snickers bar from under her baggy tee, tears open the wrapper, and bites into the nutty chocolate. Her eyelids flicker as she savours the mouthful and licks the toffee from her lips.

"I've never seen anyone eat a chocolate bar while working out before." Most women come here to keep in shape or lose weight. "What are you doing?"

"What's it look like? Keeping in shape."

"With a Snickers?"

"You don't get a figure like mine by eating salads." She aggressively tears off another mouthful with her teeth.

My eyes rake over her full figure: bouncing tits, a soft round stomach, and an ass that jiggles. Not to mention her chunky thighs. I don't have a fetish, but there's just something so sexy about watching this confident woman take a bite of the Snickers. My mouth waters, and I want to take a bite out of her.

"I refuse to lose weight because 'the camera adds ten pounds.'" She mocks the words, like she's repeating them from someone else.

"Who said that about you? I saw you on TV this morning, looking pretty fine." Fuck. I shouldn't have said that. I paste a cheeky smile on my face, one that usually gets me out of trouble, but she just gives me a death stare, as if I've just given her the opposite of a compliment.

"It doesn't matter," she says between panting breaths. "I refuse to conform to societal pressures to lose weight."

"Then why are you here at all? Why not just eat your Snickers in front of the TV?" Then my stomach turns like rotations on an exercise bike. Could she be here to see me?

Heat fills my chest, clawing at my neck. Before I get too excited, I tell myself that this is just a coincidence. She couldn't possibly have figured out where I work because she wants to get to know me.

I didn't think the treadmill could go any slower, but she taps the settings to a crawl. "I need the endorphins. I've had a bad day. And night, thanks to you."

With an opportunity to tease the feistiness in her and test my hopeful theory that she's here to see me, I say, "Are you stalking me? Funny how you show up at the park, then my apartment, and now the gym."

"Please." She snorts, lifting her chin. "Don't flatter yourself. We live in the same area. Obviously, we're going to use the same gym. Why on earth would I want to stalk you?"

She doesn't know I work here. My chest deflates like a balloon has popped. We got off on the wrong foot. Getting her to change her opinion of me is a personal challenge at this point. It's rare I meet a confident, sassy, and intelligent woman who interests me. There's something about her quick wit and confidence that I find really attractive.

"Anyway, why were you filming yourself?"

"It's for my followers."

She huffs. "Followers? What followers?"

I pull my phone from my sweats pocket and unlock the screen to my social media handle with my 1.4 million followers.

She bursts into a fit of giggles. "Lusty_Liam? You're not serious?"

"I'd like to see how many followers you have."

"Believe it or not, I'm not a prancing show pony. I actually have a brain."

I can't stop the snarl forming on my face as she dismisses me, focusing on her Snickers. It's clear Miss High and Mighty thinks she's better than me. I have no doubt she is. She might have a brain, but she's all hot air and high pressure. I'd like to teach her a thing or two.

She doesn't even know me. Who is she to judge me? She's not perfect, with her frizzy hair and opinions. I walk away but take one more look at her big ass jiggling on the treadmill. If only she would get off her high horse and get to know me, we could be perfect for each other. Opposites attract. It's now my mission to make her see there's more to me than just looks.

It's like choosing a gallon of milk; I know the whole version isn't good for me, but it tastes so damn creamy. Although, I'm not sure one taste of her will be enough to satisfy my craving. I'm gonna need the full gallon.

Six

EVE

My green dress sticks to my back as I work up a sweat on the dance floor. In the middle of the club, high on margaritas, I've never felt so free. Molly has disappeared with what's his name, but I couldn't care less. I'm out on the town, living my best life.

Being in a new city where nobody knows me is refreshing. It's as if I can reinvent myself and be whoever I want to be. And right now, I want to be the carefree girl who likes to dance like nobody is watching. People are probably watching. I've never been graceful or had any dance moves to speak of, but with my new margarita-induced confidence, I don't have a care in the world. From now on, I'm going to be unapologetically me.

A hand slips around my waist. "Can I buy you a drink?" a gruff voice says in my ear.

I spin around and smile into sparkling blue eyes. I've

probably had one too many, but a free drink is a free drink. "Sure."

He nods towards the bar with a flick of his blond hair, and I follow his lead. "What are you drinking, dollface?"

Dollface? It was going so well. "Margarita, please." I'll let that one slide.

"You look familiar. Have we met?" He hands me the cocktail.

"I doubt it. I'm fairly new here." Before sipping the fruity drink, I lick the sugary rim of the glass.

A smile slithers across his face. "Where are you from?"

"England. How about you? What do you do?"

He runs a hand through his hair. "I sell cars. I own the dealership on Main Street."

A wall of muscle presses against my back. "Your dad owns the dealership, you mean?"

"Liam, what do you want?" The blond guy folds his arms across his chest with a slight twitch in his lip.

Tilting my head, Liam comes into view. His jaw tightens as he stares off at this guy. It's as if I can't escape my neighbour. I blink a few times as I see two Liams. He's everywhere. At the park, my apartment, the gym, and now here. The universe is trying to tell me something. *Yeah, you're drunk.*

Liam tugs at my arm. "I'm taking my girl home. Are you ready to go, sweetness?"

I turn around and glare at him. "Sweetness? Why are you acting weird?" A wave of his cool aftershave catches in my nose, unlike his usual scent of leather and sweat.

"Baby, this is Bourbon, land of the weird. Let's go." He tugs my arm, giving me a stern look.

"I think she wants to come home with me, dude." The blond pulls at my other arm.

"Like hell, she does." Liam's eyes turn to thin slits.

"I can find my own way home, thank you." I yank both arms free and step forward with a light head, stumbling into a table. "Oopsies." A hiccup escapes as I say the word and stumble away on unsteady feet.

"I'll walk you home, Eve," the blond says, making me stop and swivel on my toes.

"I never told you my name. You knew who I was all along." My eyebrows pinch together, studying the smirk on his face.

Liam's hand rests on my back, causing a flurry of tingles to shoot up my spine. Well, this is new. I don't dislike the feel of his hand on me as I thought I would.

Liam holds me firmly at his side in a protective way that drunk me seems to like. "Of course he knew. He probably had some scam cooked up. Just like everything else he touches."

"I'll have you sued for slander." He fists Liam's shirt, but Liam's unfazed.

My head swishes from side to side like I'm at a tennis tournament as I take in the two of them arguing. I try to make sense of it all, but my brain's frazzled.

"And I'll tell everyone about that piece of crap you tried to scam me with. I'm sure my 1.4 million followers would like to hear about that."

Ugh, not the followers again. This guy and his fan base.

He releases his shirt with a tense jaw, his face glowing red under the club lighting.

Liam takes hold of my hand, interlacing his fingers with

mine. The tingles travel to other areas of my body. Is it wrong that I find this dominating vibe hot? Annoyingly hot.

"Don't let me catch you sniffing around my girl again. You hear?" Liam shouts as—did I even get his name?—walks off with his tail between his legs. Within seconds he's forgotten.

The way Liam says "my girl" makes drunken me all gooey. Feminist me would raise her hackles. But for tonight, I can be his girl.

Liam walks us both out of the bar and into the cool, crisp air. Another hiccup escapes, and I lose my footing on the sidewalk. My fingers cling to his biceps to stop myself from falling.

"Eve, how much have you drank?" His voice is a little harsh now we're alone, like he's my uncle.

Another hiccup. "All right, Mr. Muscle. I'm not sixteen. I'm a grown woman who's allowed a drink or two." A giggle mixed with another hiccup. "Or three, or four. I lost count after five." Hiccup.

His face turns moody as he pulls in his dark brows. "It's a good thing I showed up when I did. He would have taken advantage of you and this..." He waves a hand up and down in front of me. "This wholesome weather girl facade would have been shot to shit."

"So what now? Are *you* gonna take advantage of me instead?" I gulp, staring into his dark eyes. I almost want him to say yes. Most guys are either intimidated by me or don't want to date a fat girl. It's not often I meet a man with confidence to just take what he wants. Even if sober me hates him.

"You're not my type." He turns his head and continues walking down the street.

My chest caves. "Of course not. You like your gym bunnies." I stumble behind him with a bitter taste in my mouth. It was silly of me to think he'd be interested in me like that. I remind myself that I hate him and he still hasn't fixed my pots. "You probably couldn't handle a real woman."

He turns his head to look back at me. A curl of his dark hair hangs over his forehead. "I can handle you all right, but opinionated prima donnas aren't my thing."

With a hurt ego, I follow him, huffing behind and wobbling on my ridiculous heels. I'm not sure why his statement cut deep. I couldn't date him even if I wanted to. Dating a so-called celebrity to gain public popularity isn't me and goes against everything I've worked hard for. After years of studying my craft, I want to be taken seriously as a weather reporter, not just another fame-hungry wannabe, working her way up the showbiz ladder. "Hey. You're not my type either."

He huffs. "You don't know me."

"I know enough. You think I would fancy a self-obsessed dumb-ass like you?" I crinkle my nose as soon as the words leave my mouth. That was mean and unfair. Damn those margaritas.

He chuckles. "I may be a dumb-ass, but I can tell when someone has the hots for me, and you, frosty, can't take your eyes off me."

I'm no longer feeling bad for what I said. This arrogant arse may have a million followers, but I'm not one of them.

"You're even dumber than I thought." I stumble again on the pavement, bumping into a wall.

Liam stops walking and cages me against the brick. His brown eyes are darker than ever as they ravish my face, moving down to my heaving chest. He licks his lips, causing a strange stirring in my stomach.

His eyes flick back to meet mine. "You want me. Admit it."

Gazing into his heated eyes like a flaming Christmas pudding, I almost give in. His stubbly chiselled jaw is enough to send anyone into a frenzy. My head tilts and my lips inch closer to his. There's a weird sensation in my stomach, like a whirling wind in the fall, unsetting everything in its path.

He lowers his head. "Admit you want me, and I'll give you a taste."

Is he for real? Whatever spell he had over me breaks. Burning acid rises in my throat. I swallow, but it's no use. My entire night's alcohol consumption regurgitates all over his shirt.

He steps back, looking down at the red stains on his pristine white cotton, mixed with what looks like the odd shredded carrot. "Thanks a lot. This was my favourite shirt."

I wipe my mouth with a shaky hand, feeling a little more sober and clearheaded, but also mortified. My body heats with embarrassment, making me dizzy and another bout of sickness burns my chest.

To save myself from further humiliation, I strut off in front, summoning a small ounce of pride. "That's what you get for being arrogant."

The grumbling from behind makes me smile, knowing I've put him in his place. That'll teach him to be so bloody cocky, even if everything he said was true.

Seven

LIAM

"Aaaargh. I'm covered. How many margaritas did you drink?" I pull the shirt over my head, the smell in my nose making me gag. After screwing it up into a ball, I wipe the splatters from my jeans, then toss it into the trash on the sidewalk.

Damn this woman. Why does she get to me so much? I should have left her with Brad, but seeing them together made my stomach drop faster than a barbell. He's the sort of person who would take pictures of her in his bed, then sell them to the papers once he'd toyed with her.

Eve is at our gate, fumbling around her bag for the keycard to our gated apartment complex. With a jog, I catch her up, pull out my card from my wallet, and open the gate.

"Thanks." Her hiccups have stopped, but she looks awfully pale.

"You all right?" I push the gate open.

34

"Ugh. You're shirtless again." Her eyes roam my chest, down my abs. "What did you do with your top?"

"It's in the trash. You know, if you wanted me to strip, you only had to ask." I give her my best smile, hoping to cheer her up a little.

A white flake lands on her curls, then her eyelash. "Look at that. It's snowing." We both look up at the night sky. "It's a rare thing to get snow in Texas."

I gaze into her eyes as more snowflakes gently land on her curly hair. She softens her features and almost cracks a smile. It's as if we're in our own snow globe and time's standing still at this moment. If she hadn't just thrown up, it would be a perfect time to go in for a kiss. But I haven't had enough Dutch courage for that yet. And maybe she's had way too much.

"I'm gonna be sick again." The spell breaks as she barges past me. She retches and leans over, puking into a large festive plant pot covered in tinsel. "What do they put in those margaritas?"

Standing behind her, I hold her curls back. "Get it all up. You'll be fine. The margaritas at Loft are probably a lot stronger than what you're used to."

She retches again, but there's nothing left. I fist her hair tighter, liking how the thick curls feel in my palm. She's bent over at the perfect angle. Only a sick man would imagine what her ass would feel like with my cock inside her. And only a twisted fuck would wonder what she'd sound like if I swatted her backside. I guess I'm both, but I don't mean to be.

This woman. Even throwing up all over me isn't

enough to deter me. It's almost like a personal challenge to change her opinion of me.

"You can let go of my hair now." She stands, turning around to face me, wiping her mouth. "Were you just checking me out?"

My head snaps up. "No, of course not."

The more she resists me, the more I want her. Women flirt with me every day, but the one woman who irritates the hell out of me is the only one I want. I've never turned down a challenge, and I'm not about to start. We fight like cats and dogs, but this game has turned into cat and mouse. I will have her eating out of my hand by Christmas, her and that ginger pussy of hers.

She wobbles on her feet and I hold her steady with my hand on her elbow as I guide her to her apartment. I take the card from her hand and unlock her door with a swipe.

There's a thud in the living room, then a ginger fluff ball stretches out in the hallway, before jingling in our direction.

"Hey kitty." I bend to stroke the teasing animal. She rolls over with a purr, like a dog wanting a belling rub, her paws kneading the air as I stroke her belly.

Eve stares at the display with wide eyes.

"What's wrong?" I realise I'm in her hallway and she hasn't actually invited me in.

"Nothing. It's just she doesn't usually like strangers. When I moved here, she almost clawed Uncle Graham's eyes out." She shuts the door behind us.

Goose bumps rise on the back of my neck, aware I'm now in her apartment.

"I need the bathroom." She rushes down the hall with her hand over her mouth.

I stand in the hallway, not sure which door to go through. The proper thing to do would be to leave. But my feet won't move in the direction I want them to. I should stay and make sure she's all right.

Walking into her living space, her cat meows at the empty food bowl. "You hungry?" I search the cupboard for cat food and find a box with various pouches. "What do you want? We have salmon, tuna, sardines?"

The cat meows again.

"Sardines it is." I empty the contents of the pouch into the bowl. Diesel's gonna be pissed when he smells the cat on me. Which reminds me I have to take him for his evening walk, but not before I make sure Eve's all right.

I knock on the bathroom door. "Are you okay in there?"

She wails out a word, but I can't understand what she's saying.

"Can I come in?"

Another wail sounds through the door, so I tentatively pull the handle down and push it open a smidge before I walk through. Giving her some time to protest.

She's curled over the toilet. "I'm so ill, Liam."

"I know. Let's get you into bed." I pull her up and wrap my arm around her waist, guiding her into the bedroom. Even though she hasn't lived here long, the place looks homey, full of all her pretty furnishings.

She wipes her mouth on her forearm, then drops onto the bed with a bounce. "My pussy likes you."

I press my lips into a thin line, trying not to make a

joke. "At least someone does." I kneel at her feet to take off her shoes, then pull the covers down for her.

She climbs into bed. "You're not bad."

"You're not bad yourself." I pull the covers over her and tuck her in. "In case you don't know, nobody says pussy in the states unless you're talking about, well, pussy." A grin spreads across my face as she furrows her brow.

"So what do you call a pussycat?"

"Just a cat, frosty." I leave the room to get her a sick bowl and when I return, she's already fast asleep. Maybe frosty will warm to me after all.

Eight

EVE

My eyes widen as I take in Fitzy's apartment. Since the owner of the complex invited me to one of her many parties, I've been dying to see inside her place. Tonight's bash is in honour of her friend's cousin's nephew or something. Personally, I think Fitzy just uses any excuse for a party.

A girl greets me, "Hi, you're the new girl from England, right?" She has an English accent, too, and looks familiar.

"Yes, that's me."

"I'm Tasha. I own the bakery. Come into the kitchen. I'll introduce you to everyone." She sashays through the crowd, and I follow past Fitzy's crushed-velvet gold chaise lounge into a large kitchen with a selection of every drink known to man and cocktails on the large square island.

I always knew my uncle never used his space to its full potential and seeing Fitzy's decor gives me some ideas. Maybe I can soundproof it while I'm at it.

Fitzy's white hair is perfectly styled and the martini in her hand looks like it's stuck to her fingers as she waves it around, greeting everyone. "Welcome, my darling." Her pouty lips go in for a double air kiss, moving from one side of my face to the other. "Help yourself to whatever tickles your fancy, my dear." She lifts her drink. "Here's to naughty nights and no regrets." She has a little giggle as she wobbles away.

"Is she already sizzled?" I glance at my watch; it's only 7:30 p.m.

"That's Fitzy." Tasha shrugs.

I turn around and hit a wall of muscle. "Sorry, excuse..." My hands trail upwards over his biceps, and my eyes move towards his face.

"Fancy seeing you here." His lips curl upwards in one corner.

I immediately remove my hands. The last time I was this close to him, I was overcome with nausea. My cheeks heat at the mortifying memory. To save face, I try to make a joke. "Hi. I almost didn't recognise you with your clothes on."

"Are you disappointed?" He raises an eyebrow as if he already knows the answer.

"Don't be daft." I roll my eyes, hoping he can't actually tell I'm happy to see him here, even if I am still embarrassed by my drunken behaviour. He might annoy the hell out of me and still owe me for my plant pots, but his teasing has become a familiar comfort.

"You're not on the margaritas again, are you?"

"I'm never drinking margaritas again." I shouldn't really drink anything, but now he's here, I need a gin to take the edge off. "How come you're here? Are you following me?"

He shovels a handful of crisps into his mouth and, while he's chewing them down, he says, "I come here on the regular. I think you're following me."

"Please. I hope your dog is locked up and not rampaging through the entire complex. Have you replaced my pots yet?"

"Diesel can't help it if he's tormented by that ginger vixen."

"You males are all the same." A small smile unfurls on my lips. For all his faults, I know he's not like most guys. He could have taken advantage of me the other night, but he didn't. I wasn't so drunk that I didn't remember how he made sure I got home, and I haven't forgotten how he tucked me in.

Fitzy toddles over with her phone in hand. "Smile, you two. You're under the mistletoe."

I look up to see a bunch of the festive sprigs hanging from her kitchen lighting. Liam grimaces as if in pain, but he needn't worry. He's the last person I want to kiss. Or so I keep telling myself.

"Get closer, you two, don't be shy. You must kiss or it's bad luck," she says, waving her martini glass around.

"I'll take my chances." Liam huffs, with that grimace again and what sounds like a growl.

"Don't flatter yourself. I wouldn't kiss you if you needed CPR."

Everyone's eyes fix on us as chants of "Kiss. Kiss. Kiss." sound around the room.

I roll my eyes and let out a long sigh, then look up into his eyes that match my own hazel irises. Everything stills.

His large, rough hand gently cups my cheek. I'm mesmerised, gazing into his swirling heat. His warm lips meet mine and for a second, I forget myself. My eyes close, lips melded to his as the kitchen spins into oblivion like a hurricane taking everything in its path, but we're in the eye of the storm. Still. Just us.

His tongue slips through my parted lips, causing a strike of lightning through my centre, and I remember where I am. I push against his hard chest, breaking the kiss before it has really began.

He lets me go. I turn and scurry to the other side of the kitchen, making sure I'm nowhere near the mistletoe or Liam. I won't give him the satisfaction, no matter how much I want him.

Pouring myself a glass of gin and tonic, I glance over my shoulder. He's eating more crisps, staring at me like a lion ready to prey on its next meal. More lightning shocks fire off in my centre with each look into his eyes.

I love to hate him, but he's driving me insane. If I give in, he's won. It's a matter of pride at this point. *Pride comes before a fall.* But after he took care of me the other night, I think I've already fallen. That's the problem.

Nine

EVE

I walk into Fitzy's pantry for more snacks, looking for those cheesy crisps that everyone likes. Someone clears their throat behind me. When I turn, Liam's chest closes in on me.

My breath halts. "What are you doing?"

"Getting a snack." The pantry door closes with just the two of us in the small space. His breath lands on my cheek as he moves the hair off my shoulder, letting it flow down my back.

With no light to see, my other senses are heightened. A shiver excites me as his fingers graze my collar bone, my body betraying me again like it always does in his presence.

"You owe me a kiss. A real kiss." His thumb moves over my lips, then his hand cups my cheek as he goes in for round two.

My heart beats like the hammering of rain on a windowpane. My mind is screaming to not give him the

ANNIE CHARME

satisfaction, but my body is crying out for his attention. After several gin and tonics, my body wins. For now, it can win this battle, but it will not win the war.

Gentle lips brush mine in a teasing stroke. I let out a hum, vibrating against his mouth, and he locks onto me. His stiffened tongue darts between my pout and another moan escapes. I match his movements, taking the kiss deeper until I'm swept away in a blizzard of lust.

His free hand roams my body, exploring every curve while his other grips my head in place like he dare not let go in case I break the kiss again.

My tongue flicks against his, letting him know I want this. I need this. It's been so long since I felt this much passion, even if I hate him. *You can hate him again tomorrow*, my subconscious says.

Liam's rough hand glides under my green floral dress and squeezes my arse cheek. He stops and pulls away. With my eyes adjusted to the darkness, I gaze into his eyes.

"No panties?" he says with a cocked eyebrow.

"I'm sorry to disappoint you. I do have underwear on."

He reaches his hand farther around my backside, and I realise I've lost my knickers between my cheeks. "Ah, there it is." He twangs the fabric, pulling it from the valley of my cheeks, and runs a finger around my thigh, following the elastic of my knickers.

Holding my breath, I contemplate if I should let him do this, but my body doesn't care what my mind wants. She's already widening her stance, begging his hand to go lower.

"Is this okay?" His fingers tease at the crease where my thigh meets my pelvis, teetering on the hem of my knickers as he awaits my approval.

44

My head nods enthusiastically before my mind catches up, then my mouth runs away with me and whispers, "Yes."

When his finger crooks underneath the fabric of my lace garment, I swallow. With quick panting breaths, I look into his eyes, darker with desire, mirroring my own lustful gaze.

A finger slips between my folds into a pool of want and need. "Fuck," he whispers, then takes my mouth again, ravaging me with his lips and lathering me up in my slickness. He runs rings around me, making my walls tighten with every crook of his fingers and every flick of his tongue.

A growl vibrates into my mouth. With a grind of his hips, it's clear he's aroused just as much as I am. He presses himself into my stomach, the bulge in his denim rubbing against me. His arse moving swifter than a dog humping a cushion.

He can have me, hump me, ravish me, whatever he wants. I'm wrapped up in everything that is Lusty Liam, his fresh aftershave mixed with his own personal scent of pure man intoxicating me.

The door handle creaks. He quickly removes his hand, and I step back.

"Did you find the snacks?" Tasha says, looking between the two of us with wide eyes.

"Yeah, I did." He wipes his mouth with the back of his hand. "Best snack at this party, even if it was a little sour at first." He winks at me before grabbing a large bag of crisps and walking out the door.

My jaw tightens as I watch him leave, my body screaming for him to come back and finish what he started. I'm wound up even more than I was before.

Tasha steps into the small space. "Is something going on with you two?"

"What? No. Don't be ridiculous. I hate him." Don't I?

A different set of dark eyes watch Tasha from the other side of the kitchen. "Is something going on with you and that guy over there, because he hasn't taken his eyes off you all night." I try to deflect the attention away from myself. Seems I'm not the only one at this party who has an admirer.

Tasha glances over her shoulder into this mysterious man's one hundred degree stare and gulps like a rabbit caught in a snare.

Still dazed and horny, I walk back into the kitchen. Oh tickle my tinsel, I forgot the crisps, or did he pick them up?

Liam stands at the island. "Do you want another drink, Eve?"

I can't have another drink. I'm already buzzing from the three large gin and tonics that broke down all my inhibitions. Another drink and I'll be going to bed with him. Is that his intention? No, if it was, he would have had me the other night. "No, thank you. I'm going soon."

His eyebrows pull inwards. "You're not working in the morning, are you?"

"Yes, I am."

"On a Sunday?" He doesn't say it, but his eyes convey a hint of disappointment as they lose their sparkle.

"People still need to know the weather on weekends."

He huffs. "I can tell you the weather. Just look out the window. It's cold."

My lips lift in the corner. "I know all about how you predict the weather. Let's not go there again."

He runs a hand through his hair. "Look, I'm sorry about that. I never meant it because you're a woman. I just never met a meteorologist before."

I nod and give him a half smile. "First time for everything."

"Come on. One more drink with me. We haven't really had a chance to get to know each other."

I bite my lip to stop my smile from spreading across my face. Heat floods my cheeks. "I think you got to know me pretty well in the pantry."

He grins. "I could do with another snack. Do you want anything?"

I swat his arm. "Stop it. My resolve was weakened. Gin always makes me horny."

He raises his brow. "That's good to know. I'll make sure to buy you some."

I look at my watch. "I'm up in five hours. I really do have to go."

He places his drink on the counter. "I'll walk you back." His hand presses into the small of my back and I lean into his touch, enjoying his hands on me in that possessive way he touched me in the club. I never thought I'd like a man staking a claim to me, but surprisingly, it turns me on when Liam does it.

"I'm literally five doors away. You stay here and enjoy the party."

"You're not the only one with an early start tomorrow, frosty."

"Why? Do your one million followers demand you take your shirt off at sunrise?" I snort as I giggle and cover my mouth with my hand.

"It's 1.4 million followers. But no, I'm taking my mom to the hospital." His eyes lose their lustre again.

I place my hand on his arm. "I'm sorry. Is she unwell?"

"She suffers with MS. She has an MRI tomorrow. The doctors like to monitor how things are progressing and make sure her drugs are still working." The cocky attitude from before is gone, revealing his sadness.

He was right. I don't know him at all. But I'd like to get to know the man before me. Not the arrogant arse that he keeps acting like.

"I'm sorry." My heart aches for him. Being close with my own mother, I can't imagine what he's going through.

Fitzy is in the living room, swaying to the music, her martini swishing in her hand. I grab my jacket from the coat rack and make my way over to thank her for a lovely evening. *You should thank Liam.* What for? Getting me all hot and bothered? He left me more bothered than hot in the pantry. If you want something done right, do it yourself, is my motto.

I tap Fitzy on the shoulder, then step back as she turns around, swishing her glass of martini. "Thank you for inviting me. I've had a lovely evening, meeting everyone."

"Are you going, dear? It's still early." She takes a sip of her drink.

I look at my watch. 11 p.m. is not early. "I'm up in five hours."

She waves her free hand in the air. "Oh darling, you can sleep when you're dead. Have another drink."

I giggle. "If I don't sleep, I'll look like I'm dead."

She waves me off, and I say my goodbyes to a few of the others as I make my way to the door.

Ten

LIAM

I follow her out the door. I only went to the party hoping to see her, anyway. So leaving isn't a big deal.

"Come back to my place." The words are out of my mouth before I register what I've said.

"Ah, is that why you're walking me home, to get into my knickers again?"

"I didn't hear you complaining. Quite the opposite, actually."

"I told you already, my resolve was weakened with alcohol. The cool air has sobered me up some, so I can resist you."

We reach her door, and she pulls out her gold card.

I wait for her to invite me in. Full of hope, I lean against the door frame. "You wanted me. Admit it."

"I told you it was the gin. Are you always this arrogant?" She rests her hand on my biceps, her touch soft like a kitten, but this cat has sharp claws. "We were getting along so well and you had to spoil it."

"Were we? I must have missed that." I lean in and whisper against her ear. "Was that before or after your pussy was begging for my hand?"

"Night, Liam." She closes the door behind her, leaving me in the cold.

I chuckle to myself. This woman is so damn stubborn, like a wall of ice, but I'm slowly breaking through. She may be like a prickly icicle on the outside, but her mouth was hot like a shot of eggnog warming my belly.

Entering my hall, Diesel jumps up. "Big D. Come on, I'll take you for a quick walk. Probably the only quickie I'll be getting tonight."

The wind picks up, and the winter chill of the night air sobers me. Not that I drank much. I can't stop thinking about that kiss. We had a moment. She must be able to see that.

I'm not used to being turned down. She's definitely a challenge. I think that's why I like her. As well as her intelligence and humour, how she isn't afraid to tell me where to get off. If she'd swallow her poor opinion of me, I could stuff her mouth with something better.

I hold the lead while Diesel sniffs the same spot he's been circling for the last two minutes. "If you could hurry up and do your business, D, there might be a little bedtime treat for you." I jog on the spot to keep warm.

Finally settling amongst the brown, crisp leaves on the ground, he crouches, ears perked at the word treat.

Arriving back at my place, I get ready for bed and give D a little dog treat from his jar. Lifting the book from my nightstand, *Meteorology; A Force of Nature,* I smile. She is a force of nature. One I'd like to channel. But first I need to brush up on meteorology. Half the words in the book I've never come across before, but I want to show Eve that I understand a little about how her job is more about science than looking pretty on camera. If I can prove I take her seriously, maybe she'll give me a chance.

As I settle back against the headboard, I hear a buzzing from the other side of the wall. Diesel's ears prick up. He lifts his head out of his basket, looking around the room.

Picking up an empty glass from my nightstand, I place it against the wall. A warm smile spreads across my face, and my cock twitches when I hear a moan. The same moan she let slip against my lips earlier tonight.

I hold my breath, straining my ears to her sweet little cries and the buzzing coming from her room. My dick's rock hard.

Diesel's paws cover his eyes before dipping his head back into his basket.

"Don't give me that look."

He gets up and takes himself into the other room, and I train my ear back to Eve while palming my erection over my boxers. Is she thinking about me, like I am her? My hand slips under the fabric of my shorts, and I fist my cock, imagining her smart mouth wrapped around it.

More moans sound through the thin drywall, making my hand jerk faster. Tonight she tasted sweet, like berries, but I can't help wonder how her pussy tastes. Not Jingles. As much as I'd love to roast that ginger minx, I want to lick every inch of Eve's sweet sex until she's begging me to fuck her. I'll get her to admit how much she wants me by the end of the festive season.

Pressure builds in my stomach, causing my balls to tighten. My head rests against the wall, and I shut my eyes. Warmth spills out over my hand, filling my shorts. Fuck, that felt good.

The buzzing on the other side of the wall stops, and her sweet little moans subside. Diesel wasn't the only one who got a treat tonight.

If she wasn't so frosty, I could have been filling her up instead. She'd be moaning my name, not playing with her pussy alone. One day soon. Every cloud has a silver lining. I just need to find hers.

Eleven

EVE

"I haven't seen you at the gym, Eve," Stan says.

"I've been going." Ugh, does he expect me to go every bloody day? I have been going but I've spent more time in the gym cafe than I have actually in the gym. *Yeah, lusting after Liam through the glass partition.* A smile spreads over my face, thinking about him. Then I'm annoyed that I fancy him so much. Why does he have to be so attractive? His fit body makes him even more irritating. And, oh my goodness, that kiss.

"Are you okay, Eve?" Stan says.

I shake my head. "Yes, sorry, sir. I was just thinking about the gym."

"Eve, you're up," Dirk shouts.

I walk over to the set and stand in front of Dirk the Jerk. Funny, he doesn't have any smart-ass comment to say today, probably because the boss is here.

After work, I make my way to the gym, although I have

no intention of working out. I eyed up the cakes in the gym cafe the last time I was here, and they've been calling my name ever since.

Sitting at a small table next to the large glass wall, I peer through the glass partition, not sure why I'm searching for Liam, but when I don't spot him, disappointment weighs on my chest, making my shoulders slump.

"Can I take your order?" a young redhead asks, a bright smile pushing her freckled cheeks up.

"Can I have a gingerbread latte with an extra shot of vanilla, please? And a piece of the Texan Christmas fruitcake."

"No problem." She spins on her heel, and I turn my attention back to the wall of glass, hoping to glimpse Liam at work. He may annoy the hell out of me, but he sure is easy on the eye. Maybe he has a day off. *Maybe he's sorting out your patio.* If he has, then maybe we can be friends at least, but he hasn't even apologised, so I doubt he'll do anything about it, stubborn arsehole.

I rest my bag on a spare chair, balancing the parcel I had delivered to work, and pull out my phone to call home, hoping it will distract me. It's only been a few weeks, but I miss my family.

"Hello, my love. How are you?" Mum says. She sounds so clear, as if she's in the next room and not a thousand miles away.

"All good. How is everyone?"

"Your dad's done his back in again. I've told him to take it easy, but you know what he's like." The dogs bark in the background. "Yes, it's Eve. Awe, they must be able to hear you, sweetheart. We all miss you terribly."

"I miss you too." I rub the ache in my chest. Even missing Mum and Dad's yappy Yorkshire terriers.

"How's Graham?"

"Great. His partner, Jay, is really nice. Everyone's been really nice apart from Dirk, the cameraman who's a big jerk."

Liam stands on the other side of the glass. I suck in a breath as he walks into the cafe, giving me a wink. I turn my head away from him, but as I continue to talk to Mum, a smile spreads across my face.

"Anyway, I have to go, sweetie, the chicken dinner is burning."

"I miss your roast chicken dinners." A sense of nostalgia fills me, and I can almost smell the roast as I close my eyes. "Bye Mum, love you."

When I turn back around, ending the call, Liam is sitting at the next table, tapping the wood with his fingers. The tank he's wearing barely covers him. He may as well be shirtless.

He nods at my parcel. "Your last name is Snow?"

I roll my eyes. "Yes. I've heard all the jokes before. So please spare me."

He holds his hands up in surrender. "I'm not saying anything. It just explains why you're so cold."

Is it wrong that I want to wipe the smirk off his face with my tongue?

Leaning back in the wooden chair with his legs spread, he nods at the parcel again. "What's in the package, a new vibrator?" He chuckles. "You wore the other one out, thinking of me?"

I cross my arms in a huff. There he goes again with the

55

arrogance. "You wish. If you must know, it's a butt plug...
for your mouth."

"Oooh, kinky. I look forward to it."

What he doesn't know is I ordered him a new shirt, but
he's just annoyed me, so I don't feel like giving it to him just
yet. Besides, he never replaced my pots, so I don't know
why I felt the need to order him a new shirt.

"Are you not working today?" I ask in my most
nonchalant voice.

"You looking for me?"

"No." I squirm in my seat.

He shrugs his shoulders. His heel bounces against the
floor, making his knee shake up and down like a nervous
habit. "I saw you scanning the room. I was due a break."

"So *you're* looking for me?" My mouth lifts in the
corner, breaking into a half crooked smile I try to suppress.

"I wouldn't go that far. Don't you have some weather
reporting to do? Looks like you got it wrong again." He
points towards the window at the rain beating heavily
against the glass.

"I can only report on the data given. If anyone got it
wrong, it's the National Weather Service where the data
comes from."

He laughs. "It's so easy to wind you up."

I jut my chin. "How long is your break?"

The redhead walks over with my drink. Finally.
"Gingerbread latte with an extra shot of vanilla." She sings
the words.

I smile as she approaches, but her eyes fix on Liam,
placing the drink on his table.

My eyebrows pinch. "Excuse me. That's my order."

Liam quirks a grin, blowing on the hot drink before taking a sip. "I ordered this."

"I ordered the gingerbread latte."

"I'll bring yours over shortly, ma'am." She whisks off in a hurry, sensing my aggravation.

"But I was here first. I've been waiting ages," I yell after her as she scurries behind the counter.

"Here, before you burst a blood vessel." He slides the drink over to me.

"I'm not having that now. It has your slathers in it." I'm annoyed at the waitress, but Liam gets the brunt of my aggravation.

He chuckles. "What are you, twelve? Worried I have cooties?"

"You basically stole my drink. Do you even like gingerbread latte?"

"It's my favourite this time of year, with the extra shot of vanilla."

"Sorry ma'am." The redhead places my drink on the table, and I relax with a forced thank you before she goes back behind the counter.

I lean over the table and whisper yell, "She probably fancies you, that's why she gave you my drink."

"She's too young for me. I like my women like whiskey, a fine twenty-five-year single malt, aged to perfection." He winks at me again, causing a smile to crack my face as I blow into my hot mug.

The girl reappears, eyeing up Liam again as she walks towards him, carrying a plate with my cake.

"I'll have some of that cake, miss." He gives the redhead his best smile, and she places it on his table.

My eyes widen. "That's my order."

"I'm sorry, I'll get you another slice, ma'am." With rosy cheeks, she whisks back towards the counter.

Liam takes a large bite out of the fruitcake with butter frosting. "Delicious," he mumbles, licking frosting from the corner of his mouth.

"You greedy pig. I'm putting in a complaint about this." I give him an icy glare as he licks at more of the frosting.

He chuckles as though he's doing this on purpose to get a rise out of me. "Calm your tits. She'll bring you one in a minute."

My knuckles are practically white from gripping the edge of the table. "You didn't just tell me to calm my tits."

The waitress walks over, twisting her apron in her hands. "I'm sorry, ma'am, that appears to have been the last piece."

A chuckle sounds at the side of me, and I shoot icicles from my eyes. "I was looking forward to that."

"I'd share it with you, but it has my *slathers* on it, so..." He takes another bite, and my mouth waters.

"Fine. I'll have it," I snap. I've been dreaming of a piece of this cake all day. And let's face it, I've already had his slathers when he shoved his tongue down my throat. "I hope your hands are clean."

He slides the plate over so I can smell the spices from the fruit and the sickly scent of the buttery frosting.

Biting into it, the topping melts on my tongue. A moan escapes as I roll the sweetness around my mouth. As the buttery frosting melts away on my tongue, so does all the tension and animosity I was feeling.

Liam licks his lips. He leans over towards my table. "I love hearing you moan like that."

I stop chewing and swallow. Hairs prickle at the back of my neck where his breath whispers against my skin. Lost in the moment in the pantry at Fitzy's party, I hadn't realised I was vocal. Unless he's heard me practicing self care in my bedroom. I shake my head at the thought. It must be the night in the pantry. I hope.

He stands. My eyes wander to his grey joggers where a bulge is more prominent than before. His hand slides under the elastic of his sweats, and I can't pull my eyes away as he adjusts himself.

He hovers above me, then with his fingers curled around my chin, he forces me to look up. "Although I prefer it when you're panting." He walks out of the cafe, taking his drink with him, leaving me all hot and bothered, or just hot, or am I just bothered? I can't tell anymore.

I should stay away from Liam. We're polar opposites of each other. I couldn't possibly date a man who takes his shirt off on social media for a living, not to mention my uncle told me to stay away from him, so I assume he's a player. But there's something that pulls me towards him and makes me want to get to know him more.

The fact that he takes his mum to hospital appointments and how he took care of me when I was drunk and how Jingles rolled over for him tells me he's one of the good guys. I just wish he wasn't so cocky all the time. It's as though he puts up a shield to mask the real him. He thinks I can't see it, but the more time I spend with him, I'm certain it's all just bravado and underneath, he's maybe a little insecure like the rest of us.

Twelve

LIAM

With my phone set up on my ring light, I cover my body in oil to look like sweat—a trick of the trade—and do a few reps on the bench in the corner of the bedroom.

A few takes in and there's a pounding on my door, sending Diesel wild. His claws skid across the laminate flooring as he races to the door and back to me again. I check the time and wonder who it can be at this late hour.

Once I peer through the peephole, I swing the door open. "Eve? Are you all right?"

She pulls her robe tight around her body. "Do you think I would be here at midnight if I was all right?"

She's a force to be reckoned with. A gale force. My lip curls in the corner, knowing I can have some fun. There's nothing I like more than seeing her all huffy. "What's got your panties in a pickle tonight, frosty?"

"Can you please keep the noise down? I don't know what you're doing in there and frankly, I don't want to know, but I have to be up in four hours. So if you and your gym bunny could show some common courtesy, I'd appreciate it."

She thinks I'm here with a woman. "Common courtesy?" I bite back my laugh. A small part of me wants her to be jealous. "Oh, you want to join? You're more than welcome." I lift my arms, gripping the roof of the doorframe, giving her the perfect view of my body. "You actually look like you need to let off some steam. A good workout always helps me de-stress."

Her eyes roam my inked chest and down my abs to the bulge under my boxers, which is growing thicker in her presence.

She shakes her head, tearing her gaze from my crotch. "Are you actually covered in baby oil?"

"It keeps my skin soft. I can rub some on you if you like."

Diesel darts through my legs with a bark and tugs at the belt on her robe. She pulls it back with a grunt. Next thing, they're playing tug of war.

"Can you get your crazy dog off my robe?" Her gown falls open, revealing her little satin short set and my cock twitches.

I lick my lips, watching her tug on her belt. A waft of her scent—vanilla and dew drops—whisks by as she flaps with the robe. Diesel's gonna get a big bone for this. I silently chuckle to myself, knowing Diesel's not the only one getting a bone.

"Are you just gonna stand there?" she screeches,

wrestling with the robe.

I lean against the doorframe, enjoying the show. "You're the one on my porch. Diesel's just defending his property."

"Aarggghhh. I hate you."

"Diesel. Down boy. Basket." Diesel drops the belt and retreats inside. "I'll keep the noise down."

"Thank you." She pulls her robe closed.

"I just need ten minutes to finish off."

"Ugh. Too much information." She wobbles back to her door in her foamy slippers.

"The offer still stands for that workout. It might help you sleep better," I shout after her.

She flips me the bird before entering her apartment.

I give Diesel a good fuss. "Good boy." With a smile plastered on my face, I jump in the shower, picturing her silky shorts set and the delicate lace around her tits and how they jiggled when she was wrestling with Diesel. I recall how her nipples pebbled in the cool night air and imagine my tongue licking over her ice caps, making them melt like a snow cone on a summer's day.

Thirteen

EVE

A week passes. The festive season is in full swing. Even the gym is decked out like the North Pole. I jump on the treadmill covered in tinsel and set it at a steady walk. I also take a few selfies just to prove to my boss that I'm making full use of the free gym membership.

"Hey," Liam calls from behind me. Then he's at my side, resting on the handlebars of the treadmill, blowing the tinsel out of his face.

"Hello." I try to act disinterested and stare straight ahead.

"You working on your figure again?" He nods to the two chocolate bars resting on the screen of the machine.

I let out a small giggle. "Got to keep my shape. These curves didn't happen overnight, you know."

He chuckles. "I can imagine. I can't wait to feel those thick thighs wrapped around my waist, or better still, my ears, like a pair of warm earmuffs while I tend to your needs." His eyes rake over my body, over my arse and down my legs, making me slightly irritated and uncomfortably hot.

I pull my baggy t-shirt over my arse to hide the top of my thighs in my leggings. "That will never happen."

"We'll see about that, frosty."

My head snaps to the side. "Enough with the nicknames."

"Well, I can't exactly call you Little Miss Sunshine, can I?"

"I have a name."

"I know, Miss Snow. Very fitting, isn't it?"

I roll my eyes. "Better than Lusty Liam."

Another gym instructor pats Liam on the back as he walks by. "Liam, your appointment's here."

Dirk the Jerk walks into the gym.

"Ugh, that's all I need."

"What's wrong? You pissed I have to work now?" He chuckles.

"No, I work with him. He's a douche."

"Yeah, he's a bit of a tool. I've had to work with him all year."

"Shit in a stocking, he's coming over." I continue to walk on the treadmill. Why do I let him bother me? *Because he's tight with the boss, and you want to keep your job.* They're gym buddies and drinking buddies and probably fuck buddies for all I know.

"Good to see you working out, Eve. You know, the camera adds ten pounds." Dirk smiles as though he's just given me a compliment.

I put on a fake smile and silently curse in my head.

Liam bristles against me. "Yeah, we're just working on cardio today for optimum health. Eve looks great in front of the camera."

My mouth parts. I didn't miss how he stuck up for me then, and I don't miss how he stands at my side with a hand on the treadmill bar.

Dirk continues talking as if he never even heard what Liam said. "Liam will help you with all your problem areas. He's been my personal trainer for the last year and, well, I hate to brag, but..." He flexes his biceps and gives me a wink.

I think a little vomit just rose in my throat. Unable to speak at the sheer arrogance of this douche—who actually makes Liam seem modest in comparison—I just nod with a gaping mouth.

"I'll work on Eve's problems. Don't worry about that." Liam has a secret smile, like he's trying to tell me something.

"We're on my time now, sweetheart." Dirk taps his watch. "Liam, shall we?"

Liam gives me a quick eye roll, and I feel sorry that he has to put up with Dirk's crap, too. "I'll catch up with you later, Eve."

"Make sure you work on her thighs, Liam."

My eyes widen. I stop the treadmill. My body jolts, and I cling to handlebars as it stops dead.

Liam reaches out a hand, snaking it around my hips to steady me. "Oh, I'll work on her thighs all right." Liam gives me a smile, diffusing the anger that was ready to blow, then slides his hand over my bottom and whispers, "I'll work on this ass, too."

Tingles where his warm breath caressed my neck multiply, cascading down my spine. The feminist in me forgotten when he touches me like that.

Still whispering against my ear, he says, "This jerk's gonna pay for every dig he's ever said to you." Liam winks as he walks away and catches up with Dirk.

I'm left with a ball of words clogged in the back of my throat. Nobody has ever defended me before, besides my parents, but they don't count.

Liam and Dirk both make their way to the weights, not too far away, and I start the treadmill back up at a slow pace. It's getting late now and people are filtering out.

I unwrap my evening snacks and bite into the chocolate Kit Kat. I chew it down, willing a weight to fall onto Dirk's chest. How I'd love to shove the camera where the sun doesn't shine.

Liam must have read my mind as he adds an extra weight to the bench. He's really working him hard. Dirk's too arrogant to admit defeat. His face turns purple as he strains against the bar.

I bite another piece of the silky chocolate and savour the moment, watching my man put this dickhead through hell.

I swallow.

My man? My heart rate speeds up, even though I slow the treadmill down. Do I want him to be my man? *Clearly.* I've worked so hard to be taken seriously in my career. I'm not sure what Bourbon's wholesome news channel would make of his social media accounts. Would dating a guy like him hinder my career? Is that why my uncle warned me about him?

Over the years, I watched the weather girls date all the cliché so-called celebrities and build this B-list celebrity culture. Most of them carving out lucrative careers in show business. That's not me. I'm a meteorologist who gets excited about the weather, not red carpets and social media. I resent influencers and anyone who gets ahead because of their looks, because that's how the TV and media industry has made me feel.

People should be merited for their work and not their waistline or looks. If Liam was just a gym instructor or personal trainer, I could probably date him, but dating an influencer goes against everything I believe in.

I let out a big puff of air. There's no denying I fancy him. I can still feel his lips on me from the party. Each time I think of it, I get a flutter in my core like the rustling of leaves being swept around the park. This man is challenging the feminist in me, making me re-evaluate my principles.

He glances over at me again with a wink as he makes Dirk squat. I can't remember ever being this happy. Is it watching Dirk in pain or knowing that Liam is doing this to make him pay for how he treated me? Either way, it's a double win. I should have bought myself popcorn instead of chocolate because he's putting on a great show for me.

It's getting close to my bedtime, but I don't want to miss Dirk pulling a hamstring, or even better, breaking his wrist. I move to the exercise bike, where I'm situated even closer, and let's face it, I can sit down. I move the tension to the lowest setting, so even though I'm peddling, it's no effort at all.

The gym is empty now, apart from a few stragglers cooling off. Hopefully, Dirk will clear out soon. Although, he isn't up as early as me. He doesn't have to go through the reports and analyse the data each morning, or liaise with graphics, and he doesn't have to sit through hair and makeup.

Liam lifts the barbell from Dirk as he struggles to stand from his squat with the extra weight. I try to gauge how much weight Liam's lifting with ease as he places it back on the rack.

I usually excel at math, but trying to figure out if Liam could lift my weight and throw me around the bedroom has my brain cloud in a thick fog. Being a big girl with a height of five-foot-eight-inches, it's always been a fantasy to be lifted and handled by a strong man.

My smile pushes my cheeks up as Liam gives me another wink.

Yep. I think he could handle me.

Fourteen

LIAM

Once the session is up, I make my way over to Eve on the bike. "You're still here? Can't get enough of me, huh?"

"Don't flatter yourself. I was enjoying watching Dirk the Jerk's biceps hurt. Did you make him pay for me, or are you always that hard and tough with your clients?"

I check we're alone before saying, "That depends on the client. Sometimes I'm just hard."

Her lip curls up in the corner, and I feel myself getting turned on when she looks at me with a mischievous glint in her eye. Visions of her fucking herself pop into my head, and I can still hear her sweet little moans.

"Liam, I'm going. Are you gonna lock up?" Dev says on his way out.

"Sure. See you tomorrow." I wave him off, then turn my attention back to Eve.

"I bet you get hard for all the girls. I've seen you with the gym bunnies." Her face turns away from me.

"None of them have an ass like yours." My hand squeezes her plump cheek hanging over the bike seat.

She swats me away. "Keep your hands to yourself."

"Come on. When are you gonna stop dancing around me and admit you want to fuck?"

"I would hardly call this dancing. Don't you have a video to make or something? You haven't done your usual posing on your socials today."

I raise an eyebrow, surprised she's keeping check on my videos. "You do stalk me, then?"

A puff of air leaves her lips. "Please. I looked at your account once and now you pop up on my phone all the time. It's annoying."

My fist tightens around the handle of her bike. "Well, you're annoying. I can't turn the TV on without seeing the ice princess. Every morning is frosty with you on the screen." She doesn't need to know I only turn the TV on to watch her.

"Ugh. If I wasn't kept up all night by your hellhound, maybe I'd be in a better mood."

"Well, if you didn't keep flaunting your pussy in my face, maybe I wouldn't hound you."

"How dare you? You're the one who was grinding your dick against me."

"And you fucking loved it, but you're too stubborn to admit it."

"Okay, I admit it. Because who wouldn't want a horny dog rubbing up against them, marking their territory? What are you going to do next, pee on me?"

I know what I'd like to do. I'd love to stuff her pretty mouth with my dick.

Her tight lips press into a thin line, and she sticks her chin out. Why does she turn me on so much when she's irritated?

"I don't need to take this crap from you. I'm not short on dates."

She laughs. "I've seen you flirt with the gym bunnies, and they're welcome to you."

"What's so bad about dating me, anyway?"

"We can never date. Dating you isn't good for my image. I want to be taken seriously as a weather reporter, not a TV personality, dating her way to fame."

I huff out a small laugh. "And you think people will take me seriously as a personal trainer if I had a girlfriend who eats Snickers while exercising."

"Good thing we're not dating then, isn't it?" She swings her leg over the bike and slips, missing her footing.

I reach out and catch her in my arms. Our eyes meet. Her breath halts, and I take my chances with the brewing storm. With my arm around her back, holding her up, I bring my lips to hers. My cock jerks at the contact of her mouth and my tongue slips through the treacherous barrier, tasting the melted chocolate. I drink her in like a cup of hot cocoa on a winter's night. A fire roars in my belly, flames sizzling and crackling under my skin.

Her arms hold on to my neck as her tongue swirls around mine, adding the sweet cream to the luscious drink she is. She lets out a moan, vibrating against my lips, travelling straight to my dick. I steady her on her feet, holding her close, but a minute later, she pushes against my chest, breaking the kiss.

"It's a good thing we're not dating, because I'd have to fuck you right here," I growl.

She stares into my eyes, then with panting breaths, takes my mouth to hers again like a ferocious wind, sweeping me off my feet. My hand moves down to her big ass, and I squeeze her cheek, feeling it spill over my hand. I press her against my body. Her curves fit perfectly against my hard chest as I tease the waistband of her Lycra leggings. But they're so fucking tight. "Are these cutting off your circulation or what?"

"We're not dating. I'm not doing that with you."

"Maybe a good fuck will melt that icy exterior. I promise, my dick's warmer than your vibrator."

She swats my chest, pulling away from me. "Jeez, you're like a dog in heat."

"It's you. You make me feral." I slip a finger under the elastic of her pants.

She steps backwards. "I'm hot and sweaty and need a shower."

"Sweaty? You haven't done enough exercise to break a sweat. I've been watching you for the last hour. If anyone needs a wash, it's me."

She turns around. "I'm going in the shower." I watch her saunter to the changing rooms. Was that an invitation?

I lock the front door and turn out the lights in the gym, then make my way to the male changing rooms. The noise of the shower sounds from the women's area, and I stop at the door between the women's and the men's. This will either go very well, or it could end very badly. Have I completely misread her signals?

Fuck it.

I reach my arm behind me, tugging the tank over my head, then drop my grey sweats. Before I reach the women's showers, I'm naked. My dick stands proud, like an Olympic diver gearing up for the main event.

If her cubicle is locked, I'll head to the men's. I push on the door, and it swings open. She pauses under the water, raining down over her slick body. My eyes rake her from head to toe, mesmerised by the rivulets running over her skin and dripping from the stiff peaks of her nipples, like ice caps on a snowy mountain, melting for me?

"What took you so long?" she says with panting breaths.

It's all the signal I need to take her in my arms and meld my lips to hers. The soft mounds and curves of her body mold to my hard ridges as if we're two pieces of a jigsaw and now we're pushed together everything clicks into place.

Water rains over us both. My hand slips between her folds and fuck, she's wet. I lather her up in her slickness, rubbing circles around her little bundle that's wound up so tight. My lips trail over her jaw, down to her neck, nipping her skin as I make my way to her perfectly round tits. Taking her nipple between my teeth, I tease her, licking and sucking like I'm devouring a frozen dessert.

"Liam." She moans into my ear. "We shouldn't be doing this."

"Don't worry. We're not dating. I'm just gonna fuck your brains out. Nobody has to know."

"You want to keep this a secret?"

"Whatever you want, frosty." I pull away to look her in the eye, my fingers slip inside while my thumb still works her clit. "What is it you want, Eve?"

She lets out a sweet moan. "Fuck me. I want you to fuck me."

I knew she was feral underneath that uptight exterior. "Fuck."

"Yes, fuck me."

"No, fuck. I don't have a condom."

She scowls at me. "You're kidding. All that talk and no substance."

I slip another finger inside her. She moans as the flick of my thumb gets faster.

"I can still put a smile on your face." I take her lip between my teeth, sucking and nipping. This woman. I've blown my only chance to fuck her? She's close. Her arms wrap tight around my neck, and she runs her fingers through my hair, fisting it tight as she cries out.

"You're so fucking cute when you come. Did you know that?" Watching her nose wrinkle, and her body cling to me in a tight embrace as I work her into a frenzy, has my cock throbbing, weeping from the tip, crying out for some attention. "Turn around."

"Hmm?" She hums as she comes down from the high I've just given her.

"Turn around, Eve." I spin her, pushing her against the tiles. "Spread your legs for me."

"We can't. I'm not on the pill or anything."

"I'm not going there. Don't worry, I'm clean. You can trust me." I push my cock between her cheeks, the tip pressing against her tight entrance.

She sucks in a breath, and her body bristles. "I can't. Not there. I've never done that before."

I suck air through my teeth, my cock desperate to be inside this woman. Knowing she's never done that before only makes me want to be her first and claim a piece of her for myself, but all in good time. "Then on your knees and open your mouth, because I need to be inside you."

She drops to the shower floor, looking up at me through her dark lashes, water dripping down her face like tears. Taking my length in her hand, she angles my dick to her mouth. I brace myself, pressing my palms flat against the shower wall.

Eve may be frosty, but watching her like this is so fucking hot. Her other hand cups my balls and she massages them with one hand. Each time she flutters her lashes and moans against my dick, the pressure builds in the pit of my stomach, and as much as I want this moment to last, I may explode at any minute.

My hand strokes her slick, wet hair back off her face, and my fingers caress her full cheeks, stuffed like a hamster as she goes to town on my dick. I thrust my hips against her pretty mouth. I would say little mouth, but she's taking all of it in. And to be fair, she has a pretty big mouth when she's sounding off at me.

"Do you know how many times I've thought about stuffing your mouth with my cock?"

She squeezes my balls again, jerking me farther down her throat. I feel her gag. I can't tell if her eyes are watering or if it's the rain from the shower. Either way, I'm ready to shoot hot cum down her throat and watch her swallow her pride.

"You're so fucking perfect like this. It's the only time you're quiet." Fuck. Did I say that out loud? "I knew you'd swallow your opinions, eventually," I pant out with jagged breaths. *Stop fucking talking.*

She spits my dick out and stands in a huff with her hands on her hips. "What? Because a woman can't possibly voice an opinion?"

She's mad again. The shower turns cold, despite the hot water raining above.

"That's not what I meant, and you know it." I smother her mouth with mine, hoping I can bring back the heat between us.

She pushes me away. "Suck your own dick. I may be tempted to bite it off." She walks out, grabbing her clothes and locking herself in another cubicle.

"Eve, I'm sorry. I wasn't thinking of what I was saying. It just came out." I look down at my cock, shrivelling up like a snail hiding in its shell. Sorry, bro. It was going so well, and I fucked up.

A door slams in the changing room. "Can you let me out, please?" she shouts.

I step out of the cubicle and collect my clothes from the changing room floor where I tossed them. "Eve, I'm sorry. I should've kept my mouth shut."

She rolls her eyes, folds her arms across her chest, and taps her foot. "Yes, you should. Maybe next time I'll shut it for you."

"Next time?" Pulling on my sweats, a smile spreads across my face. "There's gonna be a next time?"

A pink blush floods her cheeks. "Er. No. We won't be

repeating this. I meant next time your dick runs away with your mouth."

The smile on my face turns to a scowl. It was good while it lasted. Fuck. I know how she felt the other night when I left her hanging. Only I haven't got a vibrator to finish me off.

"Can you hurry, please? It's late, and I have an early start in the morning." Her eyes slant at me as I find the key in my pocket.

She doesn't wait for me to lock up, and storms off to her apartment. I don't catch up. I'll give her time to cool off. She's like Jack Frost right now, freezing everything in her wake as she gusts through the cool air into the dark night.

Eve's not like the other girls I'm used to. Any other girl wouldn't have batted an eyelid at what I said, but she's different. Like she feels she has to take on the world for women's rights or something. It only makes me like her more. As annoying as she is, I'm falling faster than the snowfall during an avalanche.

Fifteen

EVE

Today has been another long day. I barely slept last night, replaying the evening's events over and over. Uncle Graham says I overreact sometimes. Maybe he's right.

With tired eyes, I slump to my apartment after work. I can't face the gym today, not even the cafe. Netflix and a takeaway with Jingles, I think.

Jingles doesn't greet me as she always does when I walk through the front door. "Here kitty. Where's my girl?"

I walk through the living area towards the patio doors. Twinkling lights glitter in the dreary afternoon. A flutter in my chest has me rushing to slide open the doors. My outdoor space is decorated like a garden centre showroom. I suck in a breath, taking in the sight of the fir garland running along the wall adorned with twinkling fairy lights. The old cracked pots replaced with shiny red ceramic ones filled with vibrant poinsettias.

A small fir Christmas tree stands in the corner, beautifully decorated with red baubles and several glittery snowflakes. My fingers delicately lift each ornament. Another snowflake has the word "Frosty" written in the centre, causing a smile to push my cheeks up so much it hurts. I stroke a glazed ceramic dove holding an olive branch.

"Peace offering," Liam says.

I spin around to face him on the other side of the waist-high wall between our patios. The aroma of herbs mixed with roast chicken floats from his open patio door through the crisp air.

"Liam, this is beautiful. Thank you."

"Come over. I'm cooking."

He knows I can't resist food. "All right. I'll be round in two minutes." Jingles appears, jumping from Liam's side. "Here she is." I stroke her and check she has fresh water. It's still the afternoon. She's not ready for her supper yet.

I walk to the front of his apartment, inhaling a deep breath as I knock on his door. He opens it with a huge smile plastered on his face. An apron with a turkey illustration and the words "Let's get stuffed" adorns his masculine frame.

I cover my smile with my palm. I want to tell him to get stuffed, but he's too adorable like this. "Thank you for making my patio look nice. It's beautiful."

"Am I forgiven?"

"Depends on how good your cooking is." Another giggle escapes me.

"Come in."

I step inside, wondering where Diesel is. He's normally

all over me by now. Following Liam into the kitchen, I can see Diesel has more important things to keep his attention, like the roast chicken on the worktop that smells divine, accompanied by roast potatoes and vegetables. "You cooked me a roast dinner?"

"Yeah, I know you said you missed your mom's roasts, so..."

"Thank you, that's very thoughtful."

"I'm actually a nice guy when you get to know me. I just say the wrong thing around you. You make me nervous."

"I make you nervous?" Doesn't he know he makes me nervous? Even now, the hairs prick up on the back of my neck when he smiles at me.

"I've never dated a girl like you before."

"We're not dating," I correct him.

"Okay, I've never known a girl like you before."

"Compared to all your gym bunnies. You mean you've never dated a fat lass before?" I fold my arms over my chest. "Is that why you cooked? You think you can win me over with food?" He probably can, but—

"Why do you turn everything I say around? You think everything is a dig at you because you're a woman or yes, have a bigger ass than some, which I fucking love, by the way."

My eyes widen. He loves my fat arse?

He steps closer. "What I meant was. You make me nervous and slightly intimidated. I don't have a degree, I barely made it through high school. You're a meteorologist, for fuck's sake. How can I compete? It's clear you're more intelligent, but not with reading people. You think everyone's out to get you." His fingers trail up my arms, leaving a delightful shiver in their wake. "Maybe I am out to get you, but only because I've wanted you since the day we met in the park. You have no idea how sexy I find a feisty, intelligent woman."

My mouth parts. Is that how he sees me? "We can't date. We fight like cats and dogs."

"I'm not saying let's date. I'm just saying I like you, and I want to fuck you. We can be friends with benefits." He brushes my hair from my face. "You're like ten of any other girl I've known before."

"In size?"

"Fuck's sake, woman. In worth." His lips crash to mine, and I kiss him back, swirling my tongue around his and savouring the feel of his unshaven jaw against my chin.

My tummy grumbles, and he pulls away with a laugh.

"Let's eat. I've even made Yorkshire pudding." He turns his attention to the oven and pulls out a tray of what I can only describe as small pancakes.

He presents them to me with a proud smile etched on his face. How can I tell him the Yorkshire pudding is a complete failure and not how we do them in Yorkshire? I can't seem to say the words. For once, I'm speechless. Probably because this is actually the nicest thing any man has ever done for me.

"They look great. This entire meal looks wonderful." I kiss his lips, wanting to reassure him I appreciate all his efforts. "I'm sorry I overreact."

He pecks my forehead. "Lucky for you, I kinda like you when you're flustered."

"It makes sense now why you're always so irritating." I

give him a smile so he knows I'm just teasing. "What can I do to help serve?"

"Nothing, you sit your pretty ass down. You've been at work all day." He pecks my nose, and it seems more intimate than the kiss we just shared.

I pad over to the dining table where I watch him serve. "Have you had the day off?"

"Yeah. I watched your report."

"You did?"

"I watch all your reports, frosty." He brings the plates over, accompanied by the Yorkshire pancakes, which make me smile.

Diesel stares at me through the entire meal, but I don't share food. This is too nice. He could probably have the Yorkshire, but I chew it down with a smile.

Liam cuts a piece up, placing it in his mouth, then spits it back out. "You English eat some weird shit."

My body jiggles with laughter. "Don't you like it?"

"No. How can you eat that?" He's still screwing his face up.

"I didn't like to say, but I don't think it's cooked properly. You need to get the fat real hot, then pour in the batter."

"What fat?"

"Did you not use any lard or cooking oil?"

"Lard? No." He gives me a blank expression.

"Then what did you cook it in?"

"The tray."

"That's why it's so anemic." Another giggle escapes me.

"I'm sorry you had to eat that. Why didn't you say? It's not like you to keep your mouth shut."

I shrug my shoulder. "You went to so much trouble, and you were so proud of them. I'll make proper Yorkshires for you one day."

"I told Mom I would make them for Christmas dinner." He laughs. "That would have been a disaster."

"Is your mum coming here for Christmas?"

"I'm going to hers. She doesn't get out much."

"What about your dad?"

"I see little of Dad. He couldn't cope when Mom was diagnosed with MS, so he took off. My sister and I take care of Mom."

"I'm sorry."

He shrugs and smiles with a mouthful of chicken. "It's not your fault. He left a long time ago. He comes to visit me when he can."

After the meal, I help clean up and load the dishwasher. "Thank you for the lovely meal. I've had a wonderful time."

"Stay." His hand takes hold of mine. "Stay longer. You're not at work tomorrow, are you?"

"No, but I have to feed my pussy...cat." I walk to the door.

He grabs my waist. "I'll feed your pussy." His lips crash to mine in a long searing kiss, making my heart race like all my Christmases have come at once.

I wrap my arms around his neck as he deepens our kiss. The heat between us rises like the smoulder in a chimney.

He takes my keycard from my hand, the gold shimmers under the twinkling lights of his Christmas tree. "Wait here."

After a few minutes, he brings Jingles back to his place, holding her in his arms. She purrs and nuzzles into his chest. "We bonded today while I was fixing your patio."

"But Diesel?" We both look to Diesel, who's wolfing down the leftover chicken. Liam places Jingles on the worktop and scrapes more chicken off the bone for her into a small dish, then gives her another stroke as she tucks in. He opens a kitchen window like I do, so she can go outside and do her business.

"You have her eating out of your hand. She likes you."

Liam kisses my nose. "Now I need to tend to my other pussy."

"Oh, which one's that then?" My voice is a little high.

His hand slides down my dress and cups between the apex of my thighs. "This one here. The one that's been weeping for my attention all night." His fingers tease underneath the fabric of my dress and tuck into the elastic of my tights. "You really are weeping for me."

"It's humid in here." I giggle.

"It's fucking tropical." His fingers slip between my folds and Diesel prods me from behind with a whine and a bark, like he can smell my arousal.

"Liam, stop."

He whips his hand away. "What's wrong?"

"Not in front of the animals." My face must be redder than Santa's coat as I feel both sets of eyes on me.

Liam takes my hand and leads me to his bedroom.

Diesel follows and scratches at the closed door. I notice his basket in the corner of the room and feel bad that he's locked out. "Will he be all right out there?"

"He's fine."

"With Jingles, I mean."

"He'll take care of your pussy, don't worry. Just relax and let me take care of mine." His fingers pull down my tights, dragging my black knickers along with them.

My heart races, knowing what's coming. "You've got protection. Right?"

"Yeah, don't worry."

I relax my shoulders as he nuzzles on my neck, then pops open each button to my dress, working his way down. As the last button pops open, the dress falls off my shoulders onto the bed.

"Spread your legs for me. Let me see your plump little pussy."

I do as he asks. Laid bare for him with nothing on but my bra. He drops to his knees on the floor at the foot of the bed. His face lined up perfectly to my aching sex.

A rumble leaves his lips. On the other side of the door, there's a whine along with a scratching sound.

Liam looks up at me with hooded eyes. "If Diesel could see me now."

I giggle, then suck in a breath as his tongue delves between my folds. He grips my quivering thighs as he circles my sensitive spot. I fist the cotton sheets, closing my eyes. When he groans into me, the vibration shoots straight to my core, making my toes curl.

"Don't move," he says as he pulls away.

I whimper at the loss of his mouth. A cool breeze blows over my naked body as he whisks to the bedside table.

He rummages through the drawer before pulling out a condom, then drops his joggers and lifts his t-shirt over his head.

The sight of his naked body never fails to excite me.

He's sculptured to perfection. The gods themselves couldn't have created a more perfect man. Only trouble is, he knows it too. He smirks, catching me ogling his chest and the black ink there, and it's the first time I've read the text woven into the intricate design.

Courage to start, strength to endure, resolve to finish.

"You like it?" he asks, rubbing a hand over his chest when he notices my gaze reading the script.

"Yes, I'd never took much notice at the words before." My eyes wander down to his full length, standing erect like a good soldier waiting to be suited up.

I lick my dry lips. My breaths come faster as I watch him roll down the rubber. The mattress dips as he climbs on board between my legs, licking me once more from my entrance to my sensitive nub and over my round stomach.

He makes his way to my face, kissing me as he moves over my skin. Tingles race down my spine like chasing Christmas lights on the patio. Hovering above me, his hand slips between us as he lines himself up for me. He inches in ever so slightly. It's been so long since I had a man like this.

"Are you okay?" He lifts his gaze to mine, inching in a little more.

"Yes." I cry out, wrapping my legs around his waist, pulling him closer until he's fully seated in my heat. "I'm not a virgin. Fuck me, Liam. I want you to fuck me."

Sixteen

LIAM

"All right. You asked for it." Damn, hearing her talk like that, so feral and out of character to her uptight, wholesome persona, drives me wild.

The pressure to perform is almost too much and my dick can't take the heat. *Don't let me down now. We're in this together.* Each time I pound into the soft mound of her plump pussy and thighs, every inch of her body molds to my rigid surfaces. She's the yin to my yang, the light to my dark. A growl leaves my lips, slipping into her sweet pussy, the syrup to my pancake.

Her little moans drive me into a frenzy. The room spins around me, like I'm in a snowstorm, and everything turns white but her. She's all I see and hear and all that matters to me at this moment.

"Liam. Harder. Don't hold back." Her nails dig into my skin. I have to hold back. If I go any deeper, I'll explode. It's taking everything I have to hold it together. Her face screws up like it did in the shower. A flash of white heat strikes between us, and I'm done for.

My movements slow to a halt before I kiss her lips and roll onto my back. "That was fucking amazing."

"Are you kidding me?" She tilts her head towards me, furrowing her brow.

"No. That's gotta be the best sex I've had in a long time."

"Are you actually done already?"

I open my eyes to see her scowling at me. Deck my balls. "You didn't come?"

"I was about to, then you stopped. I thought you were playing some sort of edging game."

How did I get that so wrong? "Let me make it up to you."

She huffs with that moody face I've grown to love. I freeze. Love? I guess I'm falling for her. I've never come so quick and hard for anyone else.

"Sit on my face."

"What?"

"You heard me." I grab her thigh. She swings her leg over, straddling my chest. My hand grips her ass. "Come closer."

She shuffles closer to my face, leaving a trail of her slickness on my skin. Hovering above me, her knees rest on the pillow on either side of my head. "Like this?" Her voice is quiet, unsure, like she's never done this before.

"Lower."

"I don't want to squash you." Her voice is weak, not the moody tempest she was a moment ago. Is she self-conscious? She doesn't need to be. I can handle a woman like her. She won't squash me.

"Sit," I growl.

"I'm not a dog." She huffs, still hovering over my face. The scent of her arousal is making me high.

"No, you're my bitch." I chuckle at my joke, trying to dissipate the tension.

She moves back, her wet pussy dripping over my chest. "I'm nobody's bitch, thank you. I don't appreciate being called one."

Shit in my sleigh. I've done it again. Me and my big mouth. I should get her to gag me next time. "It was a joke. Now come and sit so I can take care of your pussy."

She juts her chin out, chewing on the inside of her mouth. "I will sit. Only to shut you up. I might even suffocate you." She has a hint of a smile in her voice, and her eyes twinkle when she looks at me.

"Then I'll die happy." I grab her ass and pull her to my face. She gasps as my tongue pokes at her entrance and my mouth engulfs her clit.

"Liam." Holding the headboard, she rides my face like she's on a bucking bronco. Her body jerks each time I hit the spot and her legs shake.

I slip my fingers around her ass and rub the tight rosette, making her body jerk even more, and her moans become louder. My tongue works in rhythm with her grinding hips, then a gush of warmth releases from her body as her movements slow.

With trembling legs, she climbs off and collapses at the side of me with a big smile on her face. I let out a breath and lick my lips. My work here is done.

I roll onto my side and sweep the hair from her face. "Happy now?"

"Hmm." She's dazed, still catching her breath.

I kiss her nose, but she pulls my lips to hers for a deep, passionate tangle of our tongues.

"I'm more than happy." She closes her eyes. With her sex-mussed hair splayed out over my pillow and a rosy hue on her cheeks, I don't think she's ever looked more beautiful.

I climb off the bed.

"Where are you going?" Her eyes open.

"Just gonna take care of this." I point to my latex-covered dick. "And get something to clean you up. I'll be back in a minute. Don't worry. You may be frosty the snow queen, but I can tell you like warm hugs."

After cleaning myself up in the bathroom, I step into the living area to check on the animals and I'm surprised to find Jingles curled up on the rug next to Diesel, both of them fast asleep, probably in a chicken-induced coma after how much they ate.

Back in my room, I spread Eve's legs and wipe between her thighs with a warm washcloth. She's still dazed and sleepy. I toss it in the hamper and climb into bed, pulling the comforter over the two of us.

She presses against my body, squashing her tits against my chest. "Hmm, this is nice, but I should go."

Go? I hold her tight and kiss her forehead. "You're not going anywhere, not tonight."

She hums into my neck.

"Besides, Jingles is fast asleep. You can't disturb her."

Eve doesn't respond. I pull my head back to gaze into her eyes, but she's out for the count.

Seventeen

EVE

I open my sleepy eyes to an empty bed. Daylight peeks through the closed curtain. The cold air hits my body as I pull back the cover and realise I'm naked.

Memories of riding his face last night come flooding back to me, causing a smile to push my cheeks up and a warmth courses through my body despite the chilled room.

The front door opens and closes, then the skidding of claws on wood. "Diesel. Here, boy. Be quiet. Don't wake the tempest."

I open the bedroom door with the duvet wrapped around me. "Too late. The tempest is already awake."

He smiles and both boys rush over to me, Diesel getting in first, licking my feet. Liam cups my cheeks and brings his lips to mine. "Morning, frosty."

"It is a little chilly." I pull the duvet tighter around my body.

"I'll put the heat on if you're cold." His palms slide up and down my body over the duvet to warm me.

"It's okay, I'm gonna go home and have a shower." I can't resist pressing my lips against his. Warm tingles spread throughout my limbs. There's nothing I'd like more than to crawl back into bed with this man, but I have so much to do today with it being my only day off before Christmas. "Where are my clothes?"

"I hung your dress up in my closet."

I pad back into his room and open the door to find it hanging next to his shirts. He pulls the duvet off my shoulder and kisses my neck from behind. "I have to say, I kind of like seeing your clothes in my closet."

My bra hangs over the centre of the coat hanger. "Where are my knickers?"

Liam continues to nibble my neck and shoulder. I tilt my head to the side, allowing him better access and relish in his affections for a little longer.

"Your panties were a little sticky, so I put them in the wash with my clothes." The duvet drops to the floor and his hand trails over my pillowy stomach. He reaches down, sliding a finger between my folds, and I let out a moan.

"Liam, I have to shower and clean my teeth."

"Shower with me." He digs his erection into my behind, letting me know just how aroused he is.

Jingles purrs and rubs her fur against my leg, breaking the trance Liam had me under.

"Are you hungry, girl?" I unhook my bra and dress from the hanger.

"I got her some food. I stopped at the store on my morning run." Liam pecks my nose. "Go take a shower. I'll feed Jingles and cook us breakfast. Come on, girl." He walks into the kitchen, and Jingles follows, her bell tinkling gently as she goes.

I check the passage is clear before stepping out of his apartment, doing the walk of shame in yesterday's clothes. The last thing I want is for anyone to gossip when we're just friends. Are we friends? Frenemies? Frenemies with benefits. Whatever we are, I hope I get to ride his face again soon.

A tingle shoots straight to my centre each time I think of it. I can't deny he knew what he was doing, even if he misjudged the situation. He certainly made up for it with his tongue.

Eighteen

LIAM

She walks back into my apartment in tight jeans and a t-shirt. Her hair pulled into a ponytail and very little makeup. "Sorry it took me so long. I had to dry my hair."

"It's fine. I'm still making breakfast." I give the avocado another mash with the fork before spreading it on her toast.

"What's that?"

"Avocado. Have you never had it before? I thought all chicks liked this for breakfast."

"In case you haven't realised by now, I'm not like other chicks." She folds her arms across her chest. "Maybe because I'm a woman and not a farm animal." She raises one eyebrow as she lifts her chin.

I've clearly said the wrong thing again. I make a mental note to never call her anything that relates to an animal. "Are we bantering, or are you genuinely pissed? I can never tell with you. I think it's the British accent. It always sounds like you have a tone."

"Probably because I usually have a tone with you, but I get that you have no control over your mouth, so I'll forgive you." She kisses my cheek as if reassuring me this back and forth we have is just banter.

"You liked my mouth last night," I whisper against her ear.

Her smile reaches her sparkling eyes as if she's reliving it. "All right, Lusty Liam, no need to gloat, just give me the avocado. I'm starving."

"Oh, I see what's going on here. You're hangry." I hand the plate over. "Try this. Let me know what you think."

Her nose wrinkles as she takes a bite and chews it down like a dog chewing on a wasp.

"You don't like it, do you?" My shoulders slump, knowing I've failed with the breakfast.

She smiles at me as she swallows another bite, but she can't hide the unpleasant reaction to the taste in her mouth. "It's...different. What are you having for breakfast?"

I pull out my protein shake from the blender and pour a glass. "Want some?"

She screws her face up. "No, thanks, that looks even worse." Hesitantly taking another bite, her nose creases again.

I slide the plate away. "You don't have to eat it, Eve. I'll cook something else."

"Can I just have a boiled egg and soldiers? Something simple?"

I shake my head with a smile. "I should've known nothing is good enough for you."

She puts her hands on her hips. "I'm sorry that I don't like vegetables."

"Avocado is a fruit." I huff. "Didn't they teach you that at meteorology school?"

"Whatever. It's gross."

A chuckle tumbles from my lips. She's like a spoiled teenager. Is it wrong that I like her bratty attitude? "*Whatever. It's gross.*" I mock her words and watch her get more frustrated as she chews on the inside of her mouth.

"Are you mocking me?"

"Would I do that?" I smile inwardly as I secretly Google what the hell a boiled egg and soldiers are in England.

She glares at me, stroking Jingles. "Did he make you eat something nasty, too?"

Jingles purrs on her lap.

"Jingles ate up every morsel. I think she gets fed better here than at home." I hold up the gourmet tin of cat food I picked up from the store. "At least someone appreciates me around here."

"Wow, you really have splashed out. No wonder she didn't follow me home." She strokes under Jingles' chin and continues talking to the cat while I set the timer on my phone for three minutes for a soft boiled egg.

"Why do you like to wind me up?" she asks.

I ponder while cutting her toast into strips. "Because your face gets all red and huffy when you're flustered. A little like last night when you rode my face like a Texan cowgirl at a rodeo."

She squirms in her seat, the red blush I love creeping up her neck. "Thank you."

"What for? The breakfast or the riding my face part?"

"The breakfast, of course. Though I've never done that other thing, so that was a new experience."

"I'm glad I could be of service. I may not have a degree, but I'm an A student when it comes to eating pussy."

Jingles jumps from Eve's lap with a meow and darts out of the room as if she heard me.

Wanting to make Eve smile, I rummage through the kitchen drawer for a little Santa hat from Fitzy's party favours. It fits on her egg perfectly and I draw some eyes on the shell.

"Breakfast is served, my snow queen." I place the plate in front of her on my wooden dining table.

Her eyes slant before a smile breaks out. "Cute." She lifts the red hat off her egg and breaks the shell.

I sit across from her at the table, watching her eat.

"Are you not eating? What did you do with the avocado?"

"I threw it away. You said you didn't like it."

Her brow furrows. "I thought you might have eaten it instead."

"I had my protein shake."

"Wait. So you bought that just for me?"

I shrug. "It's no big deal. I just bought one from the store this morning."

"I'm sorry I didn't like it. It's the thought that counts. Thank you."

Am I back in her good books? This woman blows hot and cold more times than the east wind. I can't keep up. "What do you want to do today?"

"It's my only day off. I need to do some Christmas shopping."

"Cool. I need to go to the mall. We can go together if you like." I glance up to get her reaction.

A smile plays on her lips as she tries to act all nonchalant, dipping her toast in her egg yolk.

I silently chuckle to myself, knowing today is going to be eventful.

Nineteen

EVE

The mall is heaving with last-minute Christmas shoppers. Liam guides me towards a department store with his hand on the small of my back. It fits nicely there and each time he touches me, I get a tingle up my spine like a teenager in love for the first time.

My body halts, stopping in the doorway of the department store.

I love him?

Bugger my baubles. I can't let my feelings ruin this. Whatever this is.

"You all right?" His hand rubs at my back in small, soothing circular strokes.

I exhale, enjoying his closeness and how he puts me at ease. I nod and tilt my head to gaze into his eyes. Loving this man isn't so bad. It was inevitable from the moment I met him in the park, but there's a voice in my head telling me not to get attached. Don't get your hopes up and remember what Graham said. I make a mental note to ask Graham what he meant by that, as so far, I can't see anything wrong with Lusty Liam.

Ugh. The name reminds me of everything that's wrong. I don't want to shame him for what he does on social media, that's his choice. Though my wholesome weather girl act will take a hit if we start dating. It shouldn't matter what I do in my private life, but the public can make or break your career.

Liam kisses my temple as we walk through the store. He hasn't taken his hands, lips or eyes off me since this morning. "Who are you buying gifts for?"

"I need something for Molly. She's been such a good friend to me. I want to get my uncle something too, and Jay."

"What about your folks?"

We walk through the women's clothing section, making our way to the men's. "I've ordered their gifts online. I won't be seeing them this Christmas." My shoulders sag, wishing I could visit home. It's the first Christmas I've spent away.

Liam's brow furrows. "I thought you might go home for the holidays."

"I'd love to, but I only moved here two months ago. I haven't worked at Bourbon City News long enough to accumulate holidays."

"That sucks, I'm sorry." He stops and holds up a black lace garment, wiggling his eyebrows.

I roll my eyes. "Don't get any ideas. I won't get one leg in that."

He places it back on the rail and scans for a bigger size. "What size are you?"

I pinch my eyebrows together.

"What? I don't care. I've seen you naked and love every inch of you. Now tell me what size so I can buy your sexy ass something nice."

My breath catches in my throat. He loves every inch of me. Heat prickles my skin, despite the air-con blowing down on me through the vent. My walls clench in anticipation of wearing something nice for him and having him peel it off.

"I'm plus-size. Nothing in this section will fit."

He scans the store, then points to a sign overhead with an arrow and the words. "Plus Curves." With a mischievous grin, he grabs my hand and drags me to the plus-size section, heading straight for the lingerie.

My pumps squeak on the tiled floor as I jog to keep up with his strides. "We're supposed to be looking for Christmas gifts, not sexy underwear, you perv." A smile spreads across my face. I'm secretly loving this and hope they have something to fit me. The thought of him unwrapping me later sends a delightful shiver to my core.

"I am looking for Christmas gifts. I'm treating you, so stop your whining, woman."

"You're treating yourself more like." I glance up at him and meet his eyes. He cracks a smile, and I burst into a nervous giggle, because I'm a little hot and a little embarrassed and a little aroused each time he smiles at me.

He prowls down each aisle, and I follow until he stops at a red lace one-piece with satin bows holding it all together. He holds it up and I run my fingers through the rail, looking for my size.

I say a silent prayer when I find one big enough to fit me. Shopping for myself at home in the UK was never easy when only a few stores cater for a larger woman, but thankfully in the US there's more choice. I just wish they didn't segregate the size ranges. "Wait here. I'm going to the changing room."

"Hell no. I'm coming." Liam's arm circles my waist, tethering him to me as we walk to the back of the store.

I giggle again. "You can't come into the changing room."

"All right, but I'm waiting right here." He sits on a bench outside the cubicles. "Show me when you got it on."

"Get lost."

He chuckles as I lock the door. I would never have picked this out or worn this in a million years, but I want to please him for some bizarre reason. Feminist me would never wear something to please a man. I chew on the inside of my mouth while I undress, wondering what's happening to me. Is this what it's like to be in love?

Once I'm in the stretched lace, I stand in front of the mirror, not recognising myself, but adoring how the material feels against my skin. I hold my phone up and take a selfie of my body, then send it to Liam. Another first for me. I don't trust easily, but after getting to know him these past few weeks, he has built up my faith in men.

Once I'm dressed and out of the cubicle, Liam stands. He's on my mouth before I can even speak. His tongue pushes through my lips as he claims me with more passion than he's shown before. This is a hunger and desperate need.

I let him take what he wants, enjoying the way he devours me, a little like he ate me last night. It's funny for a man whose mouth always says the wrong thing it's his best asset when he's putting it to good use.

I pull away, breathless, and glance around, making sure no one saw us. "You got my text, then?"

He grabs my hand and thrusts it against the bulge in his jeans. "What do you think?"

I whip my hand away before we're caught. "Liam, someone could see. You're the one who told me to be careful of the press after that car salesman tried to take advantage."

"I can see the headlines now." His hand waves in the air as if picturing the headline. "*The temperature heats for Bourbon's weather girl as Lusty Liam melts her frosty heart.*"

"More like *Lusty Liam finds himself left out in the cold because he can't keep his mouth shut.*" A smile pushes my cheeks up and I give this adorable but irritating man another kiss on the lips before I place the red garment in a basket and walk to the men's section with a big grin on my face.

Liam follows like his loyal, drooling golden retriever. He's breaking down all my walls, but I'm lighter without them, as if walking on cloud nine. I just need to keep things private between us, so nothing rains on our parade.

Twenty

LIAM

I can't get the picture of her out of my head and my dick just won't go down, causing me to keep adjusting my jeans.

After helping her pick out a half decent cardigan for Graham and a glitzy shirt for Jay, we head to the food court.

Sitting on the mezzanine in a small Italian bistro, I hold her hand on the table. She pulls away, just like before, like she might catch something. "I told you, I don't have cooties."

She pinches her eyebrows. "It's not that."

"Then what is it? What are you afraid to catch? Feelings? Does the snow queen have a heart?" I lean back in my seat, tapping my foot against the wooden table leg. After how far we've come, I thought she'd be ready to give us a chance.

"I'm sorry. We shouldn't have spent all this time

together." Her head drops as she stares at her plate with sad eyes.

"Why not?" I lean forward and clench my hands together on the table.

Her fingers play with a napkin and she lifts her head, finding some hidden strength. "Because I'm falling for you," she whispers.

I relax my shoulders and let out a sigh of relief. "You fell for me that first day in the park."

Her lip curls in the corner. "I was knocked over, more like."

"Yeah, I knocked you off your feet." I run my fingers over her thigh under the table, making her smile widen.

She leans closer. "We have to stop this. It's getting out of hand. We'll get found out if we keep spending time with each other, and you keep touching me like this."

I shrug my shoulder. "Fuck it. If I lose a few followers for having a girlfriend, so what?"

Her head drops. "Because you have a fat girlfriend?"

"I didn't mean it like that." I lift her chin to look me in the eye. "Why do you always think the worst? I meant because some of my following are gay men."

"I'm sorry. You're right. I always take things the wrong way. I'll try not to."

"Why is that?" I can't help wonder what happened to her, to make her so defensive.

She lowers her coffee, clattering it against the saucer with her shaky hand. "Because nobody ever wanted to date me growing up. I was always the chubby nerd."

Something cracks in my heart, seeing her vulnerable. I want to take her in my arms and worship her body, show her how beautiful she is. "It doesn't change what's on the inside."

"When I was younger, I tried every fad diet going. I tried so hard to fit in at my old job in the UK, just to have a chance of actually being able to give my own weather report on camera. Then one day, I just thought this is ridiculous, realising it's society that needs to change, not me."

This explains a lot. "Is that why you hated me?"

"I never hated you. But yes, I hate what you stand for on your socials." She puts on the voice of Derek in *Zoolander* as she says, "There's a lot more to life than being really, really, ridiculously good looking?"

A laugh bursts from my lips. "Wait. You think I'm ridiculously good looking?"

She laughs along with me. "You know I do, but I hate that pretty privilege is a thing. People should be merited on talent, not looks."

"You know, I think you're the full package."

"You're one of few people to say that." Her eyes sparkle under the restaurant spotlights.

I lean closer, so only she can hear. "Let me tell you something. The reason nobody wanted to date you is the reason I want you."

Her hazel eyes widen and sparkle. "You want me because I'm a chubby nerd?"

"You know, my favourite type of *Nerds* are the chubby kind. They're the juicy ones full of flavour." I quirk a grin, stroking her thigh with my knuckles. "But candy aside, I want you because you're intelligent, and I find your big ass sexy as hell."

A red hue tints her cheeks, and every time she goes shy on me, my cock twitches.

She looks up at me through her thick lashes. "I like you too. I won't say why, because your head is already big enough. But looks aside, I like how you make me feel. When you're not saying the wrong thing. But I just want to keep things private between us."

"I can live with that." For now. I may have my body plastered all over social media, but when it comes to my family, I am a private person. My fans don't need to know about my personal life and, frankly, I don't think anyone would actually care about my family's struggles. If Eve wants a little privacy, I can respect that, but there's only so much sneaking around I can take.

Twenty-One

EVE

By the time we get back from the mall, it's late.

"I have to take Diesel out for his walk. Put that red outfit on and get yourself ready for me." Liam pecks my nose before disappearing into his apartment, and I enter mine.

I give Jingles fresh food and water, even though she isn't around, probably at his place, waiting for the gourmet tuna Liam enticed her with. Padding into the bathroom, I freshen up and put the red lace underwear on for him. Although I have no idea why he insisted on buying this for me. We both know it won't stay on long.

He lets himself in and puts the catch on the door. I hear the claws on wood and smile, knowing Diesel is with him, followed by the tinkling of Jingles' bell.

The bedroom door opens, and I pull the cover over me, wanting to make Liam wait a little longer before he sees me in his gift.

Liam closes the door. His dark eyes are hot on my skin, like the sun's rays burning through the clouds. "Are you ready for me?"

I nod, unable to speak, watching him strip down to his boxers. He fists his length under the fabric of his shorts, then grips the duvet and pulls it away, letting it drop off the foot of the bed.

His mouth parts as he takes in the sight of me in the red lace. "You look like Santa's naughty little helper in this outfit."

I gulp. Anticipation bubbles in my veins. My stomach churns like the brewing of a storm as lightning crackles in my chest.

He loses the shorts. "Tell me, frosty, have you been a bad girl?"

Taking in the sight of him, my mouth waters like I'm staring at a huge Snickers bar, veins and all. I gulp again as he crawls on the bed. "I'm a good girl."

He hovers above me, tugging at the ribbon over my nipple, hiding my stiff peak like wrapping on a gift. "You want everyone to think you're good, but I know deep down you're bad." His gruff voice has my body aching for him.

I scooch down the bed slightly and lift my hips, needing to feel his erection between my thighs.

He lifts, denying me the friction I crave, but nibbles at my neck instead. "Such a greedy pussy you have."

"Liam, don't tease me." I moan, tilting my head to the side so he has full access to my skin. Lifting myself up, I rest back on my elbows, letting my head roll back as his searing mouth moves south over the lace.

With his teeth, he takes the ribbon tied into a bow

covering my nipple and tugs, opening the slit over my breast. My pebbled nub pokes through. He engulfs me, sucking hard on my peak. With each stroke of his tongue, I imagine it elsewhere and my walls clench.

Another moan bursts from my lips. My hips gyrate, seeking the friction I need to quench my desire. "Liam, please."

He tugs at the ribbon on the other side and frees the other nipple, giving it the same love and attention as the first. "What do you need, frosty?" His hands hold my wrists, pinning them back on either side of my head.

"Your mouth." I pant the words. Thunder rumbles in my chest as I moan again.

His mouth, dripping with lust, makes its way over the stretched lace on my stomach until he reaches the first bow on my pelvis. He pulls it open with his teeth, exposing the triangular tuft of hair and kisses me there, before moving down to the next one. "Is this where you want my mouth?"

Lightning sparks in my centre. "Yes," I say with short gasps of air, desperate for his tongue.

"Spread your legs for me." His breath lands on my sensitive area, sending a delightful shiver up my spine. He pulls at another bow, exposing my slick opening.

I gasp as his tongue pokes my entrance, then licks upwards to my bundle of nerves. "Liam, please. Just fuck me."

He lifts his head and gives me a sinister grin. "You are a bad girl. You need to be patient. All good things come to those who wait."

This is pure torture. I want, no, I need him inside me.

With each stroke of his tongue, my walls pulsate. "Liam, please."

He flips me over, leisurely taking his time, undoing each bow on the slit that runs all the way to my behind. Exposing my bottom, he kisses my cheeks and moves lower to the next one.

This is another first for me. Nobody has ever paid so much attention to my arse before, and I can't deny I'm up in the clouds. Light moans escape me as I lie blissfully on my front. With each caress of his lips and each stroke of his fingers over my skin, I sink deeper into the mattress, enjoying the pleasure he's giving me.

He hovers above me, spreading my cheeks. His erection presses against my tight rosette, and I gasp. His lips caress my back as he moves my curls to the side and he whispers into my ear, "Where's your vibrator?"

My eyes widen. I turn my head to look at him. "Why? Are you planning on coming too soon again? You need a backup?"

His body rocks against my back as he huffs out a laugh. "It's a possibility. I can't control myself with you. Where is it?"

My face flushes. "I don't have one."

He huffs another laugh. "What do you fuck yourself with then, your toothbrush?"

"What are you talking about?"

"I've heard you, Eve." Not believing me, he reaches over to my bedside drawers, rifling through each one.

I gasp for air. "Heard me?" My face heats; lava claws its way up my neck, ready to explode with embarrassment.

"Here it is." Liam holds up my pink glittery vibrator

like he's carrying the Olympic torch. He presses the button and watches the rotating head and the little bunny ears buzz, chuckling to himself.

I cover my face with my palms, heat radiating off me like a toasted marshmallow.

He turns off the vibration and kisses my cheek. "Don't worry, frosty. I was right there with you. Every time you moaned, I stroked my dick faster until we both came together."

I jab him in the ribs with my elbow. "What?"

"At least I think we came together. Unless you just ran out of batteries."

I pinch my eyebrows. The fire in his eyes conveys all his truths.

"Lube?" He rummages in the drawer again and pulls out the blue tube.

"I don't think you need the lube. I'm wet enough."

His thick finger slips between my thighs and he grunts out, "Sleigh balls. You are. But it's not for there."

I gasp when he drips the cold gel on my ass and massages my tight hole. "Liam, I told you. I've never done that before."

"On your knees. You may be the brains here, but I can still teach you a few things."

With shaky legs, I lift, holding myself on my elbows. My head dips onto the cushion as he works a finger into me. I push back, enjoying the strange pinching sensation.

The buzzing of the vibrator thrums at the apex of my thighs and I jerk as he presses it against my nub. His finger teases inside me, loosening me up for the main event.

"Liam, will it hurt?" I don't know why I asked, because

at this point, I don't care if it hurts. I want him to fill me up and use my body however he likes. Him taking what he wants from me is the sexiest thing I've ever seen in a man.

"If it does, I'll kiss it better afterwards." He removes his finger and lines himself up, the tip of his length pressing against me and he inches in slowly.

My fists grip the sheets, and I push back against him. The vibration still on my sensitive area takes my mind off the burning sensation he's giving me.

His hand grips my hip. "Good girl. You're taking me so well."

I tilt my head, gazing into his eyes behind fluttering lashes. "I thought you said I was a bad girl?"

"Oh, you're so bad, you're good. You're what every man wants." He thrusts into me hard. "A good girl for everyone else, but bad between the sheets."

With each thrust, the burning desire intensifies, making me moan and push back to take him deeper. I whimper when he moves the vibration away from me, but suck in a breath as he pushes the rotating head into my slick opening.

"Liam." I pant, tingles firing through every limb as he stretches me to the hilt. My head is about to explode. I've never felt so full of deliciousness.

"Yes, Eve?" His hand fists my curls, pulling gently, but with enough force to lift my head off the pillow. "Tell me you love this as much as I do."

"Oh, gosh. Yes," I cry out as he works the vibrator in rhythm with his dick.

He groans into my back as his lips press against my spine. "Since the night I had you bent over, holding your hair, I've thought about having you like this."

My mind is a haze of thick lust, like a fog I have to wade through to gather any logical thought, but I know what night he's talking about. "The last time you held my hair like this, I was throwing up."

He ploughs into me with a punishing thrust. "Yeah."

"You were thinking about this while I was ill? You sick fu—"

Another punishing thrust has me biting my lip, and the fog thickens, scrambling all previous thoughts.

Liam groans, pushing in and out of me at a steady pace. "I'm gonna need you to come for me. I don't know how much longer I can keep this up. You're so fucking tight."

I bury my head in the pillow, everything turning black. All I focus on is the heat between us. The rabbit ears find their way to my sensitive nub as he pushes the vibrator in farther, making me jerk. Lightning strikes my core. With my eyes screwed shut, flashes of white fill my head, and I cry out in blinding ecstasy.

"Good girl." With his powerful arms, he scoops me up, bringing my back flush with his chest.

My body pulses around him, gripping him and the vibe as my muscles clench and throb with aftershocks.

He bites my shoulder and pinches my nipple. A groan rumbles from his throat as he comes undone. His body trembles against mine. I'm limp and boneless, held up by his arms, holding me against a wall of muscle.

Still breathless after the dizzying high, I rest against him. He kisses the sting on my shoulder with hot ragged breaths escaping his lips.

The vibrator slips out of me, falling to the bed, humming gently against the sheets.

We stay like this while we catch our breath. His lips brush against my ear as he whispers, "I want to be the man to give you all your firsts." He kisses my neck. "The first man to have you ride his face." He kisses my ear as he whispers against me, "The first man to fuck your ass." He sucks my shoulder. "The first to show you how a real man treats his woman."

I'm trembling in his arms, but not from the cold. His warm body against me is all the heat I need, but his words are what send a shiver through my core. Now I've had a taste of what he promises, I want more.

"Wait here. I'll get something to clean you up." He lets me go, and I collapse into a heap on the sheets. As if I can walk after that.

A dreamy haze clouds my mind. I can still feel the ghost of him inside me. My body thrums with aftershocks from the earth shattering orgasm. I'm ruined now for all other men. How can anyone ever top that? Not even a battery-operated boyfriend could top that. I glance down at the humming vibrator on the bed, knowing it's now redundant unless I'm with Liam.

A warm cloth swipes between my cheeks causing me to suck in a breath. I hadn't realised he meant he was going to wipe my arse. "Is it messy?"

"I've wiped Diesel's ass many times. Yours is much prettier, trust me."

"I hope you don't shag Diesel up the arse, too." I clutch the pillow with both hands and cringe as he continues to wipe me.

He chuckles. "Only bad girls get this attention." He throws the cloth in the hamper and rolls me onto my back.

Hovering above me, he kisses my lips delicately, like I'm a china doll that he's just broken and glued back together.

"And how many bad girls have you been with?" I hold my breath, wishing I hadn't asked that question. I don't actually want to know how many girls he's had.

He drops to the side, slipping an arm under my head, and pulls me close to him. "Not many. I don't sleep around."

I lift my head. That wasn't what I expected him to say. "You do plenty of flirting."

He smiles. "Are you jealous?"

"No."

"It's hard being in my position. I never know if a girl likes me for me, or for my money or my fame."

"I've never had to deal with that before. It never occurred to me until the other week when you rescued me from that car salesman that someone might just want me for their fifteen minutes of fame."

"Seeing you with him made my stomach churn." His jaw clenches, and I stroke the stubble there, kissing the tension away.

"You have me now. You don't have to see me with anyone else." What am I saying? We're not even a couple. This was only ever meant to be just sex.

He pulls me closer and holds me tight against his chest, showing me he feels the same.

I don't know if I'm ready to commit and then there's my uncle telling me to stay away from him. But there's nowhere else I'd rather be than wrapped up in Liam's arms.

Twenty-Two

LIAM

I missed Eve this morning. She starts work at the crack of dawn. Instead, I wake up to Diesel licking my face. "All right, all right. I'll take you out." I throw the duvet off, and pull on my jeans and t-shirt from yesterday.

Walking into the hall, I smile when I see Eve's note and keycard.

I'm free later if you are. Last night was amazing. Can't wait to do it again.
Eve x x x

Damn, I miss her already. I thought nothing would beat getting her all huffy and agitated, but seeing her warm smile is surprisingly even better. She's like salted caramel, both salty and sweet. I'm not usually this sappy, but I want to do nice things for her all the time. Seeing as she's not going home to visit her folks this Christmas, I wonder if she'd like to come and meet my mom.

No, it's too soon.

Mom would love her, though.

She's always asking when I'm going to meet a nice girl. I think she means a Southern belle, not an English rose. But being with Eve is like drinking top-shelf whiskey when I've only ever sampled vodka.

I clip Diesel's leash onto his collar and walk around the park, thinking of what to do tonight. I should take her out. Yeah, I'll book us a table at the little Mexican joint. She'll love that, and I can ask her about her plans for Christmas. Surely she can get a few days off during the holidays.

Back at my apartment, I turn on the TV while I make breakfast like every morning, just to see her face before starting work. Drinking my protein smoothie, I can't stop the grin when she appears on my screen.

She's glowing. I don't think I've ever seen her this happy. She really enjoyed last night. I must have dislodged that stick up her ass.

Her bright smile makes everything seem sunny, even if she is talking about a cold front sweeping in from the north.

Later at work, Dev comes over. "Hey, Liam. That chick you like is in the cafe."

I glance at my watch and then to the cafe window to see her smile and wave. Holding my hand up, I signal for her to give me five minutes to finish with my client.

"You're hot for the weather girl, man?" Leo, my client says, handing me the dumbell.

"Yep, she's my girl." I freeze, almost dropping the weight. I want her to be my girl. After last night, I can't see her turning me down.

"She's sweet." He hands me another dumbell to put on the rack.

Sweet? He didn't see her last night. She was anything but sweet. I'm getting hard just thinking about her wrapped in red lace.

I focus back on Leo to stop the thoughts of Eve taking over. "How's things with you and goth girl?"

He frowns at me. "Her name's Olive. And I'm working my way into her good books." A laugh bursts from his mouth. Then I get the joke. She owns Ravens bookstore. "Laters, man."

I bump fists with Leo and can't get into the cafe fast enough.

Eve's sitting with a latte—gingerbread by the smell of it —and a piece of fruitcake with butter frosting. I sit opposite her and grab the cake, taking a big bite.

"Hey. Get your own."

I chuckle. "Sorry. Couldn't resist. Just like I can't resist doing this." I lean over and lift her chin, kissing her lips.

She pulls away. "Liam." She gives me a pained look while checking her surroundings and wiping my kiss from her mouth.

"What's wrong? You weren't pulling away last night." My chest tightens. Has she had a change of heart?

She leans over the table and whispers, "Not in public. Someone might see."

"I don't want to keep us a secret anymore. I want everyone to know you're my girl. What's wrong with that?"

Squirming in her seat, she says, "Nothing, I just think we should keep things private."

I lean back in the chair, straightening my spine. "Are you embarrassed to be seen with me?"

"It's not that." She glances around the cafe, looking anywhere but at me.

"Then what? If I was a doctor or a lawyer, I don't think we'd be having this conversation." I shift in my seat, clasping my hands together.

She leans over and whisper yells, "A doctor or a lawyer doesn't take their shirt off for likes and follows. I don't want our private life all over the media."

"Well, I'm sorry I'm not good enough for you. You talked about not having to change yourself, but you're asking me to change who I am. I've made a career from my socials. I can't give it up; it's who I am. I don't want to give it up." I wave a hand in front of me. "If you can't accept that and accept me, then you're not the woman I thought you were." I stand, screw the napkin into a ball, and throw it on the table as I walk out of the cafe, more pumped up than I've been all day.

Of all the people who've made me feel like I'm worthless over the years, I never thought she'd be one to add to my list. I hang my head low as I stomp over to the treadmill to let off some steam. When I turn back to the cafe window, she's gone. So much for our plans tonight. I'll have to cancel the booking.

Twenty-Three

EVE

I haven't seen Liam for a few days. He wasn't home when I called round his place to apologise. My regret's been lodged in my throat ever since, reminding me I was wrong. The truth is, I let fear ruin what we had. The fear of standing out with a man like him. Fear of the tabloids, as well as his fans, criticising me for dating out of my league.

I'm not blind. I know I'm punching above my weight with him. He's ridiculously good looking, with a body to match. It's taken me years to accept my body and now I need to accept that I deserve to be loved, too.

I miss him. Is it so bad if people know about us? What's the worst that will happen? My uncle has a moan about how he warned me about him but never actually said why. Or a few people say I'm dating my way to fame. So what? I've worked hard and have the degree to prove it. I shouldn't worry about what people think.

Bourbon's wholesome news station can't say much, he's only taking his shirt off. It's not like he's showing off the crown jewels. This is the twenty-first century. Surely people can't shame him for showing his torso.

If he's willing to risk his following, then I should risk something, too, even if it's the public onslaught of being out of his league in the looks department. What I lack in brawn, I make up for in brains. We complement each other perfectly.

After work, I head to the gym, seeing as I can never catch him at home. Even Diesel has been quiet.

I change into my leggings and a t-shirt and walk around the gym looking for him. He's with a client. A woman. I sit on an exercise bike with my bag of goodies.

He's laughing at something she's said. My heart sinks, watching his hand go to her hips as she squats. When she bends her knees for the third time, our eyes meet.

I swallow the lump of chocolate down as he stares at me with sad eyes. Could he have been hurting like me this whole time?

The brunette distracts him and his hands go back to her waist. He takes his eyes from me and focuses on her arse.

I tear off another bite of chocolate and slump on the handlebars, hoping I haven't blown my chance with him. How stupid of me. I had this amazing man, and I shot him down.

He's flirting with her now. I can't hear what they're saying over the music, but their body language tells me everything I need to know. The way he bites his lip when she sticks her chest in his face and the way he positions his hands on her arse. The chocolate rises in my throat, and I swallow it back down with another piece.

Finally, the session is over. She writes something down on a piece of paper and hands it to him. He smiles and runs his hand through his damp black hair, lifting it from sticking to his forehead.

Once she's out of the picture, I swallow my pride and walk over to the bench where he's tidying up the weights. "Hello."

"Hey."

"I haven't seen you at the apartment for a while."

He shrugs. "I've been busy going out with friends. People who aren't embarrassed to be with me."

Another girl approaches him. "Are you ready for me, Liam?"

He gives her a smile. A smile that only last week would have been for me. "I'm always ready for you, darlin'."

I walk away, deflated. Not wanting to torture myself anymore, I gather my belongings and head home.

The shirt I bought him sits wrapped on my kitchen table where it's been all week. Another reminder of him. I open the cupboard looking for the cheesy crisps, or chips, as he calls them, then collapse on the sofa.

Barking from the patio makes me jump, and I wipe the cheesy drool from my mouth. If Diesel's outside, Liam must be home. I grab the gift and slide open the patio door. "What's all the fuss about?"

Diesel jumps up, resting his paws on the wall between our patios, and I give him a good ruffle behind his golden ears. "Have you missed me? It's good to know someone has."

"I've missed you too," Liam says with a raw voice.

He stands behind Diesel, shirtless, making me shiver in the nippy December air.

A smile spreads across my face. I hold up the wrapped gift. "Peace offering."

"You got me a gift?" He takes the parcel.

"Open it."

He tears the wrapper. "A shirt?"

"I figured you might need one if you're gonna be my date to the BCN work Christmas party tonight." I hold my breath, hoping this will show him I want to showcase our relationship to the world. What better way to come out than at the news station's party, and with my uncle there too?

He rubs the back of his neck. "I actually made plans tonight."

"Oh." I release the breath I was holding. My chest deflates like a popped balloon. "Keep the shirt. You might need it to take your gym bunny out." I spin on my heel, my heart imploding. What did I expect? I've been stubborn. Now he's giving me a taste of my own medicine, playing hard to get. If he wants to be that way, then fine.

My eyes swell like the sea before a tsunami, but I won't allow myself to cry. This is my own fault. I've been stupid and wrong, trying to protect my reputation as well as my heart.

Taking in a deep breath, I pick Jingles up, giving her a stroke as I make my way to the living room to crash before tonight's festivities. Stroking my pussy always soothes my heart.

Twenty-Four

EVE

Jay hands me another glass of champagne. BCN has spared no expense at this Christmas bash. We're at the studio, but it looks different, decked out to the nines and with as much free alcohol and food as you can eat. A singer too. Some famous country singer I've never heard of, but Jay's loving it. With the cowboy hat and Wranglers, he fits in well. He takes my hand, trying to cheer me up by giving me a twirl. Graham shakes his head at him and sips his champagne.

"Liam, nice shirt," Graham says, lifting his champagne flute.

I spin on my black heel, facing a wall of muscle covered in a white shirt with a small present print. My gift. "You're here."

He runs a hand through his gelled black hair, pulling it back from his forehead. "I'm here. If you still want me."

My heart thumps in my chest, as if warning me not to mess this up again. "I thought you had plans."

"Well, when I put your ridiculous shirt on, the only person I wanted to unwrap me was you, so..."

I giggle, knowing the shirt is ridiculous, but he pulls it off well. "A ridiculous shirt for a ridiculously good looking man." My palms slip around his neck and pull him to my lips.

His hands slide around my back, hugging me close against his chest. I hope this will prove to him I don't care who sees us together. I want him just as he is, and I'm willing to add him to the long list of things I will fight for.

He deepens our kiss, devouring me in front of everyone as if breathing oxygen for the first time. Gripping my shoulders, he pulls back with a big smile on his face, then he lifts me, spinning me round. I catch Graham giving Jay an odd look, but I don't care. If Liam's wrong for me, then I don't want to be right.

"Dance with me." Liam leads me to the makeshift dance floor when the singer sings "Frosty the Snowman."

I swat his chest. "Did you ask her to sing this?"

He chuckles and pulls me to his chest again as we sway to the music. "It was this or 'Let it Snow.'"

"You know, I missed you so much. I even missed you making fun of me." I wrap my arms around his shoulders. My fingernails stroke the back of his neck as he smiles down at me.

"So, are we official? Are you ready to be my girl?" His nose brushes against mine and I hum in approval.

"I am. Come rain or shine, I want the world to know you're mine." I relax in his arms, knowing things are going to be okay between us. It's also a relief to have things out in the open with Uncle Graham.

Glancing around the room, all eyes are on us. "What do you think they'll make of us?" I ask Liam, clinging to him like a life raft in a turbulent sea.

"You don't have to weather the storms alone, frosty." He kisses my forehead. "Whatever they think or say, we'll deal with it together."

"I was too afraid of what people would think. Especially now I'm in the public eye, but I like you just the way you are. I don't want you to change."

His lips peck my nose. "Is it too soon to say the three little words, frosty?"

Warmth spreads through my body. Any frostiness I had left has well and truly melted. "What three words are those, lusty?"

He bursts out laughing.

I swat his chest again. "What? You chose that hideous name yourself."

"It just sounds weird coming out of your mouth." He pecks my lips again.

"All right, I'll just call you my man, then."

"I like the sound of that." His lips press hard against mine.

My tongue darts into his mouth, swirling around his heat, mouth watering with desire. He's tastier than any drink served at this party.

"How long do we have to stay at this party for?"

I pull back to gaze into his eyes. "You just got here."

"I need to have you, Eve." He holds me close so I can feel his arousal.

I lift on my tiptoes to whisper in his ear, "Come with me." I drag him out of the room and sneak off down the dark corridor to hair and makeup. We burst into the dressing room where Lisa works her magic. Liam flicks on the mirrored lighting illuminating the room.

"I don't have a condom."

"I got the shot last week. I'm good to go. Unless you've been sleeping around. If you have, tell me, and I'll get protection."

"I swear, I haven't touched anyone."

He doesn't know how much I needed to hear that. I kiss his lips, unwrapping him as quickly as I can. He falls into the dressing room chair, and I hike my green dress up, then slip off my knickers before straddling him, desperate to feel him unwrapped between my thighs.

"Damn, you really have missed me."

I smile against his mouth, rubbing my slickness against his length. "Shut up and kiss me."

He doesn't need telling twice. His large hands grip my plump behind and force me down on his hard dick.

A moan escapes me as I slide down his chimney. "Christmas has come early." I trail kisses down his jaw, moving lower to his neck as I ride on his sleigh. With each rock of my hips, my walls tighten around him.

He yanks my dress down at the front, letting my breasts spill over the fabric. His mouth engulfs my nipple, and I let out another moan.

Twenty-Five

LIAM

I can't take it any longer. The slow rock of her hips isn't enough. I need to pound her hard and fast. Gripping the cheeks of her ass, I stand with her in my arms. She sucks in a breath, clinging to my neck as I spin her around, laying her in the chair. Her eyes dance with wonder as I pull a lever, tilting the chair back then plough into her at the pace I need.

"Liam. Yes. Fuck me. Harder."

When she talks dirty like that, I swear my cock thickens more. "You asked for it." I thrust deeper into her, watching her eyes shut tight. Gripping her thighs, I lean back and look down at my dick entering her plump little pussy. Her little button on display just asking to be pressed. "Wrap your legs around me."

Her thick thighs have me in a vice as she holds on, taking my rapid thrusts, and I move my thumb to circle her swelling clit.

"Liam." Two circles later, her channel clenches around me. Her body jerks, her back arching. Unwrapped, I can feel every pulse of her pussy.

My balls draw up, and my stomach tightens. "Eve." Coloured lights cloud my vision. I thrust into her again, emptying my sac. My legs shake against her vibrating thighs.

She lies limp in the chair, catching her breath, red lipstick smeared all over her face, but she's never looked more hot.

I lean down, scooping her up in my arms, and bring her pretty face to my lips. When I got dressed tonight and looked at myself in the mirror, wearing the shirt she bought me, I had to come and claim my girl. I know how hard it was for Eve to swallow her pride and apologise, and I didn't want to waste any more time.

"I'll get something to clean you up." Scanning the room, I spot the tissue and a sink in the corner.

She takes the tissue from me and cleans herself, then sits up. "Oh no. I look like a clown."

"Good thing we're in the makeup room."

She wipes the lipstick off her face and starts applying some powder. "You go back to the party. I'll catch up with you when I've sorted myself out."

I kiss her forehead. "I'll see you out there."

"Where did you get to? And where's Eve?" Jay asks. His shirt is even more hideous than mine with gold baubles embroidered into the fabric, matching his golden highlights.

"She's just in the ladies' room." I grab a glass of champagne from a tray and down it in one swallow. I'm parched after that workout.

"What's going on with you two? I hope you won't hurt her." He furrows his brow, waiting for an answer.

Hurt her? I fucking love her. Hurting her is the last thing I'm going to do. People always assume the worst of me. Because of my social media rep, they assume I'm a player. Just because women flirt with me at the gym doesn't mean I take them up on their offers.

"I'd never hurt her." I take another drink from the tray as Graham walks over and places his arm around Jay. My old neighbour never liked me, but I need to get on his good side to pursue a relationship with his niece.

"Nice to see you again, Graham." I lift my drink to my lips, my throat more dry by the second.

Graham nods as he sizes me up. "So, you and Eve are a thing? Funny, she never mentioned you before."

"We wanted to keep things quiet."

Graham folds his arms over his broad chest. The guy's bigger than me, like a grizzly bear ready to crush anyone who hurts his niece, but he doesn't know I'd do the same. "If you hurt her—"

"Liam, what are you doing here?" Stan says, walking over with a whiskey tumbler in his hand.

"I'm with Eve."

He bumps my fist like he's trying to be cool. His usual greeting at the gym. "You and Eve? I never would have thought it. We could use this to our advantage. The public would love it. Local heartthrob, Lusty Liam, bags local weather girl next door. His very own Christmas Eve." He waves his hand in a rainbow as if writing out the headlines in the sky.

"No problem. I'll even give you an interview." I lean in closer. "Can I ask for a favour?"

He puts an arm around me as he leads me away. "Anything for you."

"I wanted to do something nice for Eve over Christmas, but she says she hasn't worked long enough to earn time off."

"You want me to give her some time off?" He takes a sip of the whiskey, then swirls the ice around, rattling it against the glass.

"Yes sir. If that's possible. I want it to be a surprise."

"How can I deny young love? Call the office tomorrow, tell HR what dates you want, and I'll get them to approve it." He hands me his business card. "I want our studio to run this story first."

"Thank you, sir."

"Ah, here she is." He looks over my shoulder with a beaming smile. I turn to see my woman in her emerald gown with a smile that lights up the room like a Christmas tree.

"I'll leave you lovebirds to it." He walks away with a little dance singing, "Let it snow, let it snow, let it snow."

"He's in a good mood." She kisses my lips lightly, making sure she doesn't ruin her freshly applied lipstick.

"I have that effect on people. You seem to be in a good mood, too. I wonder why?" I wrap my hand around her waist and pull her to my chest.

"It may have something to do with this super fit guy I

was with in the dressing room." Her cheeks blush and she looks down with a giggle.

"Yeah, tell me more. I want to hear all about him."

She strokes my biceps. "He has muscles for days. A gorgeous smile." She pulls the hair back from my forehead and moves her hand over the stubble on my jaw. Her eyes peer into mine. "But more importantly, he's kind, thoughtful, and loving. He cooks too. I wouldn't change him for the world. Maybe we can work on your Yorkshire pudding, but other than that—"

I crush my lips to hers. All I've ever wanted is for someone to love me for me and not because of my followers or solely for my body. Eve sees me, the real me. "There isn't a thing I want to change about you, either."

Twenty-Six

EVE

J ay sits opposite me in the canteen, taking a break from graphics. "You never told me you were dating the lord of lust."

"His name's Lusty Liam to you." I smile at the silly social handle I've come to love.

"Yeah, I know. Lord of lust is just what his fans nicknamed him. His other handle is liamthelustytrainer."

"He has another account?" I mumble with a mouthful of my sandwich.

"It's kind of like a fan club where he sends out a newsletter to all his subscribers."

"Wow. Busy boy." I take another bite of my sandwich. Pride swells in my chest. I never knew how dedicated he was. He must work really hard to manage that on top of his daily posts and working full time at the gym.

Jay chuckles. "He is quite the busy bee. Don't worry about your uncle. The only reason he doesn't like Liam is because he's jealous. I used to follow Liam and when I started dating your uncle and saw he lived next door, I was kind of fangirling about him."

My eyes widen. "You fancied him?"

"Duh? Have you seen him?"

A smile spreads across my face, feeling a little special that I've actually seen him naked in all his glory. The entire world may have seen him flexing his pecs on social media, but only I get to see him intimately.

"He's actually a really nice guy. Your uncle would know if he bothered to get to know him."

"So all this time, he's been telling me he's bad news, all because he thinks you fancy him?"

He chuckles again. "Yeah, I'm sorry. Ever since he saw his newsletter on my laptop—"

"Why? What was so bad about his newsletter?"

"Jay, Celia's asking for the graphics overlay for the game this afternoon," a colleague says.

Jay nods. "I've gotta head out. Invite Liam to dinner next weekend. Don't worry about Graham, I'll talk to him."

"Thank you. That means a lot. You guys are the only family I have here." I take another bite of my sandwich and pick up my phone. My fingers tap into the Google search bar "Liam the lusty trainer."

There he is on page one. Impressive.

How did I not know he had a website? A very intricate website, too. Large images of him in calendar poses fade in and out on the home page, making me smile. A feed of some of his videos with millions of likes run along the footer.

Knowing I get to go home to this man—kiss his lips while running my hands over his inked chest—gives me butterflies in my tummy.

I click on the shop link and let out a giggle when I see he actually has a calendar. Wow, there's so much merch. Water bottles with gym slogans, gym bags, clothing. I'm super impressed. He must have someone manage this for him. I want to meet him or her. Is it wrong that I hope it's a him?

A newsletter subscription pops up. What the heck? I type in my email address, "headintheclouds1..." I can't think of anything better than reading his newsletter on my lunch break.

Sure enough, I get a welcome email with details of his paid subscription if I want the gold package. This guy really knows how to sell himself. I knew he backed himself, but this is another level.

A pop-up box appears on my screen with a gift box. The words "Unwrap Me" dance across the screen, followed by "Only $5." Okay, what's five dollars? I tap the icon and with my index finger pressed against the fingerprint recognition button on my phone, I've paid in seconds and confirmed my email address.

Wondering what I've unwrapped, I wait for another email, a naughty smile stuck on my face as I wait for pictures of my man.

Ping.

I'm almost giddy when an email pops up titled, "Unwrapped For You" in the subject field. Clicking open, a Merry Christmas message and then the top of an image of Liam under a shower appears. It looks like his bathroom in his apartment, but I can't be sure. I'm not exactly focused on the background. His head is tilted back, with a hand running through his hair. Water droplets cling to his body like diamonds cling to rock.

Using my thumb, I scroll down to see more of his glistening body. My eyes pop when I get to the part where he's fisting his erection. With a racing heart, I scan around me, making sure no one can see what I'm seeing, even though anyone with five dollars can see what I'm seeing.

Swallowing hard, my throat is excessively dry and scratchy, with a pulse bursting out of my neck. His dick is on display for all to see. The next image is of him in bed, clearly a selfie and he's smiling, his leg bent to the side, the covers over his other thigh and his hard cock poking out from under the covers with the head covered by a little Santa hat. I gasp, zooming in with my finger and thumb. The same little Santa hat he used on my boiled egg.

Why is he doing this? How could I not know he does this? Tears form in the corner of my eyes as I hyperventilate. Another image of him at the gym. He's taking a selfie again in the mirror. His grey joggers pulled down enough to show the V that points towards his not-so-private area, but his very public area, it would seem. How many people have paid for these photos?

Underneath there's a message.

Click here to subscribe, and get weekly unwrapped pics direct to your inbox. Only $20 a month.

It's not even a one-off. It's a monthly subscription. He clearly doesn't need the money. Does he? A hundred scenarios go through my head, trying to understand why he would do this. I trusted him.

My heart sinks. I thought I was special being the only one who got to be with him intimately. Despite the world seeing his pecs, I thought I was lucky because only I got to see the rest of him.

How can I take him home to meet my parents? If they found out. And work. If anyone here found out, or the press. My cheeks burn like a heatwave in the Sahara desert.

"Eve, they're waiting for you."

I glance up at Molly, remembering I have a job to do. With shaky hands, I turn my phone off and slip it into my bag before making my way to the set.

I've never been so nervous to see him before. My heart is in my throat. I don't know what to say. Opening the door to my apartment, Jingles is the first to greet me, rubbing herself against my leg, then Diesel jumps up at me with his tail wagging. I give them both a good ruffle. When I look up, Liam is in front of me.

"Good day?" he says with a smile before pecking my lips.

I stand frozen, then clear my throat. "It's been eventful."

"Oh yeah. What happened?" His smile dissolves when he sees my eyes swelling up like a cumulonimbus cloud. "Eve, what happened?" His hand grazes my cheek as he furrows his brow with a deep line of concern etched on his magnificent face.

I don't want it to end. It's been going so well, but with

this new revelation, I feel betrayed. Did I even know him at all?

His lips kiss my forehead. "Tell me what's up, rainbow."

Rainbow? The lump in my throat is the size of a bauble and my stomach twists like tinsel tangled on a tree. We've only just begun and now I'm about to end it, but I can't date a guy who shares dick pics with the world. I can live with him shedding his shirt, but this is a whole new level.

My hand slips into my bag to retrieve my phone. His email is still open. I hold it up in front of my face with a trembling hand, displaying his full erection in the shower. "This is what's *up*."

He stares at the screen in my hand, then back at me. "You subscribed to my newsletter?"

"Yes. I got the unwrapped special edition."

He huffs out a half laugh. "You didn't have to pay. I would've sent you them for free."

I slam my phone on the sideboard. "For the price of a coffee, you may as well be handing them out for free. I didn't realise you were so cheap." It takes everything I have not to burst into floods of tears, although the anger in me boiling up is most likely evaporating any swell of moisture.

"You think I should charge more? I like to keep my prices low. I think I get more takers, but if you think it's too cheap, I can talk to my agent."

"Are you serious? You're missing the point here. Are you completely stupid?" As soon as I shout the word stupid, I regret it, but he isn't taking this seriously.

The concerned wrinkle in his brow turns to a scowl. "Forgive me, I'm not as fucking clever as you, Miss Fucking Frosty Forecaster with your four-year degree."

"I trusted you. At work, I'll be the laughing stock. I could actually lose my job."

"Why? Because the wholesome weather girl isn't so wholesome after all? Perhaps they'll discover you like to be fucked up the ass, too."

"How dare you? Are you blackmailing me?"

"Don't be ridiculous. I actually love you. Fuck knows why."

My heart dances, hearing the words I've longed to hear. "I don't want us to fight."

"Then what do you want, Eve?"

"I want you to stop with the naked pictures."

"I can't. I make too much money with them, and too many people are relying on me."

"There are more important things than a fancy rich lifestyle."

"It's easy for you to say that, isn't it? We haven't all got rich uncles who work in the TV business, handing out jobs on a plate. I've worked hard to get where I am, and I'm not giving it up."

"I can see exactly how *hard* you've worked by looking at your dick pics. Real fucking HARD, Liam. If it's money you're worried about, move in with me."

"Are you gonna pay for my mom and sister, too?"

I shake my head in a huff. "What have they got to do with it? Do they know what you do? I'm sure they're really proud of your weekly newsletter."

His jaw tenses. "They don't know the full details."

"How much money do you actually make?"

"About five grand a week."

My eyes pop. I do the figures in my head. "$260,000 a

year from dick pics?"

He shrugs, trying to do the math. "If that's what it adds up to."

"Okay, sign me up, too. That's five times more than what I earn doing weather reports."

His head flinches backwards. "What are you talking about? Sign you up for what?"

"Ask your agent to set me up with a website and an account. I'll sell naked pictures too. We'll be minted."

"You're not serious?"

"Why not? Surely there's a market for a fat lass like me. I mean, you couldn't keep your hands off me, so..."

"No fucking way are you doing that."

"Why not? Too embarrassing for you? Don't want everyone seeing just how chubby my thighs are or how squidgy your girlfriend's stomach is?"

He clenches his fist. "You know that has nothing to do with it."

"Then why can't I do it? It's clearly working out so good for you."

"Because I'm not having other men jerking off over your tits, that's why."

I scream through gritted teeth, "Exactly. Don't you think this is how I feel? My uncle's boyfriend used to subscribe to your newsletter, for goodness' sake. If you want to continue having a relationship with me, you need to stop sending out pictures like this."

"I told you I can't. Too many people are relying on me."

"I'm sure your fans can get their fix elsewhere. There must be a million other people willing to sell their body."

"Are you shaming me?" His eyes narrow, his jaw clenching as he breathes heavily through his nostrils.

"No. I would never shame anyone for sex work if that's what they enjoy or that's what they need to do to survive. I admire the confidence it takes to do this sort of thing. Don't you get it?" I close my eyes, summoning the strength I need. Tears pool under my lids. "I want to be the only one who gets to see you like that. I don't want to share you with the world and I certainly don't want my family or colleagues finding naked pictures of my boyfriend."

"Are you done?"

"If you won't stop, yes, I think we're done, don't you?"

"Diesel. Here, boy."

Diesel whines and follows with his head down as Liam stomps out the door. He turns around. "If I'm so much of a fucking idiot, why were you dating me?" He slams the door behind him, making me shudder.

Did I overreact? I don't think I did. He wasn't even interested in stopping. The look on his face as he walked away sticks in my head like the TV on pause. My throat closes up as the emotion chokes me. I know I hurt him, calling him stupid. I hate myself for it now. Of all the things I could have said, I don't know why I used that word. I don't think he's stupid at all. I was very impressed with his business sense, just not the product he was selling.

We're polar opposites of each other in every way. It would never have worked, but why does it hurt so much? Emptiness suffocates my lungs like a nothingness taking over, making me numb from the inside out. What have I done?

Tears drip from my lashes. The cumulonimbus clouds

condensing to a torrential downpour. I walk into the kitchen, inhaling the ginger from the oven. I turn it off before it burns and open the door to a selection of ginger cookies he's made for me.

Why does he have to be so stubborn? He'll come round won't he? I'll give him a night to cool off, then I'll apologise for calling him stupid and he'll apologise for...for being stubborn, for not telling me he sends dick pics, for wanting to keep his fans happy instead of me.

I dry my tears and take the tray of ginger cookies to the bedroom, where I have every intention of staying for the rest of the day.

Twenty-Seven

EVE

It's the Friday before Christmas. I should be taking Liam to my uncle's, but he's disappeared off the face of the earth. The day after our argument, he wasn't home when I finished work. I tried calling him, but it just rings. He's still posting on his socials, so at least I know he's okay. I guess I deserve the silent treatment. I just want to apologise for overreacting, although I'm still not sure I did. What girlfriend wants their fella's naked pictures plastered all over the internet? I'm still hoping he'll come back with his tail between his legs, but at this point, I think it's fair to say we're done.

Jay opens the door to his home. "Come in." He wraps me up in his arms and kisses my forehead. I've confided in him this week. He says he can understand both points. Who would want to give up all that money?

Although I don't know what Liam does with it. Yes, our apartments cost a pretty penny, but he didn't exactly splash out on much else. His wardrobe mostly consisted of gym clothes and hoodies. He owned the odd nice pair of trainers, but other than that, he lived a fairly basic life. He probably splashed out more on my patio than he had on his own Christmas decorations.

Spaghetti bubbles in the pan, an Italian aroma filling up the kitchen as Uncle Graham stirs the Bolognese sauce. "How's it going, hon?"

I shrug my shoulders. "I'll be okay."

"Here, have a glass of red. You're off work until the New Year. You can relax." He pops the cork in a bottle of wine and reaches for a glass.

"I'm back Boxing Day. Then I have New Year's Day off."

Jay looks at his timetable pinned to the kitchen notice board with a puzzled look on his face. "You're definitely off work. You booked holidays in. I have the schedule."

"I definitely have no holidays booked. If I had, I would've gone home for Christmas. I didn't think I would get any holidays with me starting so close to Christmas."

Jay pulls the schedule up on his phone and my name is crossed off. "See. If you didn't book the holidays, who did?"

I grab my phone from my bag and fire off a text to Lucy in HR. "Someone has made a mistake. Some poor soul wants Christmas off, and they put my name down instead."

"Maybe." Graham serves the spaghetti Bolognese, his signature dish. Not very Christmassy, but I'm not exactly in the festive mood.

We sit at his fancy dining table that's reserved for guests. I'm sure they rough it with dinners on laps in the lounge when it's just the two of them.

"Still not heard from him, then?" Jay asks.

"Nothing." I stare down at my spaghetti, all messy and tangled, a little like my life right now. "He's ghosting me."

"His mum lives in Reagan Springs about an hour away. He could've gone home for the holidays," Graham says as he adds parmesan to his dish.

"Yeah, his colleague at the gym said as much. I just wish he'd answer my text." Forcing myself to eat, I twirl the spaghetti around my fork and take a bite.

"You could always send him a message on his socials," Jay says with a bright smile.

"And let the world see our business? No thanks. He's obviously not that bothered. I mean, if he was, surely he would have been in touch." It's not a bad idea, but I find it hard enough to swallow my pride, let alone make a public apology.

"Not if he's still hurt. It sounded brutal from what you told me." Jay takes the parmesan from Graham before he uses it all.

"Okay, don't rub it in. I already feel bad about calling him stupid." It's usually him saying the wrong thing. I wasn't thinking. I was so angry and shocked, I didn't even register what I was saying until it was too late.

I know he puts on a bravado and this cocky attitude to mask his insecurities. Confidence shows competence and while he has many amazing qualities and a knowledge of things that I know nothing about, he was insecure about his lack of education.

I could have called him anything and it perhaps wouldn't have stung so much as the word stupid. The truth is, I'm the stupid one. Instead of acting like a tempest in a teacup, I should have listened and talked to him about how I feel in a calm way.

After dinner, I help Jay load the dishwasher.

"Eve. Eve, come quick," Graham shouts from the living room.

I slump in, wiping my hands on my jumper. Graham stands facing the TV with the remote in hand like he's seen a ghost.

"What is it?"

"It's Liam." He points the remote at the TV and sure enough, Liam's sitting on a red sofa, holding hands with an older woman.

"Turn it up. Can you rewind it?"

He rewinds the show. A pop culture weekly news show, *Hyped*. I drop to my knees on their plush rug in front of the warm glowing fire and TV.

Jay walks in. "What's all the fuss about?"

"Shh," we both say in unison.

The presenter announces Liam and his mother, Laurel, and the crowd clap as she hobbles on set, Liam holding one arm, with a crutch under the other.

I remember Liam telling me about his mum's MS, but I hadn't realised just how disabled she was.

The presenter continues to talk as they sit down on set. "Liam and Laurel, welcome to *Hyped*. You've been creating quite the storm in recent weeks with all the charity work you've been doing. Tell us a bit more about that."

"Charity work?" Jay says.

"Shh."

Liam holds his mum's hand. "When Mom was diagnosed with MS, none of us had heard much about the disease. We didn't know what to expect. As Mom deteriorated and became worse, my sister moved in, able to work part-time from home, allowing her to be Mom's primary caregiver. She's sacrificed a lot of time, money, and her life basically to give Mom the help and care she needs. I felt helpless, living over in Bourbon, but I found a way to make a bit of extra cash to support Mom and my sister, and I made sure they were comfortable."

I glance at my uncle and Jay with tears in my eyes. All this time, he's been doing it to support them. I wish he'd told me. Maybe I would have understood why he does what he does. I I may not have liked it, but knowing it's for a charity, I could have helped, donated even.

The presenter says, "How did the charity work start? Tell us how you got into that."

"My brand took off on all the social media apps and what started as me talking about fitness quickly became me taking my shirt off, and each time I did a shirtless video, my views went through the roof. I started making money from my videos and getting endorsements. Then I set up my website about this time last year."

It's been going on for a year?

"I didn't know what to do with the extra money. Growing up, we learned to live a simple life, and now I was making quite a lot of money and sending it home."

His mum chimes in. "I told him we didn't need this much, but he wouldn't have it, saying, buy yourself something nice. Well, I visit the centre each week with others in my position. It's run by a lovely group of volunteers who organise bingo, coffee and cake mornings, things like that. It was a lifeline for me, but they didn't have funding to keep the centre running, so I started the charity with the help of the volunteers and the spare money from what Liam would send each month, and we kept the centre going."

"Such a fantastic story, and now you've been able to build a brand new centre through your charity that you recently named, 'Every cloud has a silver lining.' How did the name come about?"

"It was inspired by a friend, actually." He has a sad smile, making my heart ache. "When the forecast is bad, it is important to find something good."

"You've certainly brought the silver lining to everyone's hearts this Christmas with your generosity. $250,000 is an amazing gift that will go towards helping others like your mom who struggle with MS and other debilitating illnesses with nowhere to turn."

"I just want to say that all I've done is donate some money, and the real heroes are those people that volunteer their time, day in and day out. People like my sister at home taking care of Mom twenty-four seven and the volunteers at the centre who keep the communal space running, so people have somewhere to go, and others to talk to who are in a similar situation."

"I think you're all unsung heroes and of course, up to now, you've been a secret Santa, quietly donating on the side, until a member of our team uncovered your story after clicking on your unwrapped newsletter." She giggles. "Will there be more to come?"

"Nah, I'm not doing the unwrapped boxes anymore. Although I'll still be doing my newsletter but my future pictures will be all wrapped up. I just want to save the unwrapped for that special someone."

Jay gives my shoulder a squeeze.

"Before you go, can I ask if you have a significant other? A certain weather girl that may have inspired the name, perhaps?"

His foot taps against the floor, something he does when he's nervous. I hold my breath, wanting to place my hand on his knee to settle his nerves.

"Nah, we're just neighbours."

"That's a wrap. Thank you for coming on *Hyped*."

Just neighbours? Not even friends. I rub the ache in my chest. He's been going through all this alone. He told me about his mum having MS and I never really thought to help him in any way. I should have asked more questions and talked about it more. Maybe he would have opened up about this.

I realise now that none of this was a secret, just that I was too wrapped up in myself and my own issues to ask more about his family.

My phone buzzes, startling me. The show cuts to an advert, and I tap the screen when I see my boss's name flash across it. "Hello?"

"Eve, what's going on? I've just watched the crew from *Hyped* interview your boyfriend. We should have had that story. How does it look when one of our own is on a rival station?"

"He's not my boyfriend, and I didn't know any of this."

"You two seemed pretty cosy last week at the Christmas party."

"We broke up the next day." There's a wobble in my voice. Why didn't I listen to him? It all makes sense now. He said he couldn't stop because he didn't want to let anyone down. He knew he was donating the money.

"You broke up?" Stan's voice rumbles through the phone. "But the next day he was calling HR, wanting to book Christmas off for you, said he had a big surprise planned."

"He booked my holidays?" I gasp, lifting my head to Graham and Jay as they hover next to me, listening to the call.

"Yes. I only agreed because I thought it may help your career and the company. People love a romance. Bourbon's weather girl dates Lusty Liam, media superstar. The press love all that."

"He made his money selling naked photos. I didn't think you'd want that kind of publicity."

"He's hot property right now. Publicity is publicity."

I can't believe what I'm hearing after all the spiel about how Bourbon News is a clean, wholesome station that people rely on. "But this is a family station?"

"Yes and this is for charity. Haven't you seen *Calendar Girls*? Surely you've heard of them, weren't they from the UK?"

"Of course I have." I glance at Jay and Graham who are just as wide-eyed as me, hanging off every word from our boss. "It doesn't matter now. I can't even get in touch with Liam." Tears sting my eyes. If only he'd acknowledge my messages. The thought that he's ghosted me stabs me in the chest.

With a formidable tone, Stan says, "Maybe it's time you got creative. And when you do, call me. Merry Christmas, Eve."

The line goes dead before I can protest. With teary eyes, I look up at Jay and Graham. "I have to go. I need to get my best dress on and post a video on social media. Hopefully, he'll respond to that. I have to tell him how sorry I am."

"You go, girl." Jay clicks his fingers, and Graham chuckles, rubbing his beard. "I'll call you a cab."

In the taxi home, I think about what to say on the video. I miss him; I miss Diesel too. Jingles misses him. She's been off her food all week. But there's no way in hell I'm selling a story to my boss, whatever the outcome.

Once home, I set up my phone on the mantle next to the Christmas tree, all set to record. Jingles jumps onto the ledge, her ginger fluffy tail in front of the lens, then she knocks my phone. It falls into the tree in slow motion. I hold my breath, hoping it's intact.

Reaching down underneath the tree, I delve between two presents I'd wrapped for my uncle and Jay. And there's another gift there that I don't recognise. *Frosty, my Christmas Eve* is written on the small package, wrapped in a ribbon with a red bow.

My heart pounds in my ears. The whole time this has been here. Is this the big surprise he had for me? I sit on the floor and unwrap the reindeer paper. A printout of two tickets to England, flying out on Christmas Eve.

I'm a hot mess, a puddle on the floor of my living room, unable to string together two coherent words through my sobs, let alone do a bloody video. He did this for me, but he isn't here to see my reaction. I want to hold him and tell him I was wrong, that I want to be with him and I'm sorry. I don't understand if he's stopping with the naked pics, why hasn't he called me? That's all I wanted from him.

With blurry eyes and a sniffling nose, I prop my phone up on the hearth and press the record button.

My eyes are puffy. Black eyeliner runs down my cheek and the angle of the camera is all wrong, highlighting my double chin, but I don't care.

"Liam, I've just unwrapped your gift." I hold the printout up and wipe my nose on my sleeve. "I'm sorry. Please call me, even if it's telling me how stupid I've been. You always said I was the intelligent one, but I've been a stubborn idiot. Will you forgive me? I love you." A smile breaks through my tears like a ray of light breaking through the clouds on a rainy day.

"Yes, I love you, and I don't care who knows. I want the universe to know how much I love you. I'm going to use these tickets to England. Tomorrow, I'll be at the airport, catching the flight, and I'll be waiting with your ticket. If you don't come, I'll understand, but I really hope you'll be there and let me be your Christmas Eve."

With another sniffle, I press the stop button and upload, not even bothering to play it back. I've had an account on this video app for a while, only to stalk Lusty_Liam, but it's my first post. I tag his handle in the video, hoping he'll see it. His account must be blowing up after being on national TV, so I'm not holding out much hope.

I call Graham and Jay for moral support. They offer to take Jingles while I'm away, then I pack.

Twenty-Eight

LIAM

"Cheer up, love," Mom says as she fusses over Diesel. I can't tell if she's talking to me or the dog. We've both had a face like a smacked ass since we arrived here.

My sister walks into the room and places the phone back in its holster next to Mom's recliner chair. "That was another reporter, Liam. You can answer the phone next time."

I lift my head from my slumped position. "What did they want?"

"They want the inside scope on your relationship with the weather girl." She rolls her eyes as if she's disappointed in me for how I've handled the situation.

I'm disappointed in myself, but I don't regret what I did, only that I should have told Eve from the beginning, but it's not something you blurt out on a first date. *Hey, by the way I sell naked photos online. I can send you some if you like.* Nobody likes unsolicited dick pics.

"She wants nothing to do with me. It's over." I take a sip of my breakfast smoothie, playing events out in my head and wondering if I could have done things differently. I wonder if she watched the *Hyped* show last night. Everyone else seems to have seen it, based on the onslaught of reporters calling.

"Maybe you should have been honest about what you did for a living." My sister raises an eyebrow. "I'm still a little shocked myself. My phone hasn't stopped with messages from my friends, Liam."

I tilt my head in her direction. "I didn't know you had friends."

She whacks me over the head with the back of her hand. "Careful. I still have those chubby photos of you when you were twelve."

A chuckle escapes. Probably the first time I've laughed since I got here. Not even my morning run with Diesel has cheered me up. I know what I did was for a good cause and I stand by what I did to raise the money, but the way Eve looked at me and called me stupid made me feel worthless. The last time I felt like that about myself was when I was the fat kid in the photos my sister mentioned, and being bullied at school for being dense. I might struggle with learning, but exercising was the one thing I could control and it became something I enjoyed.

My phone vibrates from the coffee table like it has all morning. I watch it silently shake against the wooden surface, the screen lit up like a Christmas tree with every app showing a notification. Normally, I can't wait to check my socials. It's the first thing I do when I wake up and the last thing I do before bed, but I can't bring myself to look at my phone. For two days I've let it sit on Mom's coffee table, slowly draining the battery.

"Are you going to answer that?" Mom says, nodding at phone.

I lift my feet and rest them on the coffee table, knocking the phone in the process. "Nah, it's just a notification. Or probably another reporter wanting a story." Since I came out so to speak on *Hyped*, it's like the press have gone mental this morning. I didn't even say anything about Eve, other than she's my neighbour. I can't understand why the whole of Texas has gone nuts over this. Don't they know she hates me?

"How do you know it's not Eve trying to call you?" my sisters says.

A huff escapes my lips. "She barely called me when we were dating. She definitely won't be calling me now. Besides, she hates me, remember."

"I'm sure she doesn't hate you, love." Mom presses the button on her electric chair. Slowly, it lifts her from her sitting position. "Nobody could ever hate you."

My sister smirks. "I could."

I glare at her. "I can return the spa weekend I've bought you."

"Be nice you two." Mom shuffles in her chair, now in an almost standing position. "Pass me the walker, love."

I position it in front of her so she can grab ahold as she stands. "I can get you what you need, Mom."

"Can you go to the restroom for me as well?" She smiles

with a shake of her head as she shuffles across the room, her slippers sliding against the carpeted floor.

My sister drops into the spare chair opposite Mom's recliner. "Mom's worried about you. We've never seen you this upset over a girl before. Or is this the first time you've ever been turned down?"

"You're loving this aren't you?" I glare at her smiling face. The twinkling lights from the Christmas tree reflect in her glasses.

"I'm sorry. But yes. I like the sound of anyone who can stand up to you and put you in your place, Mr. Me and My Two Million Followers."

"1.4 actually." I throw a cushion at her smug face. I don't miss the chuckle in her voice as she lifts her arms to shield her face.

Diesel lifts his head, then drops it again on the plush rug in front of the heater.

Mom shuffles back into the room, gripping her walker. "Shall we turn the TV on?"

My sister holds the remote control and points it at the TV. "There must be some Christmas movies on or something. Might even cheer up misery over there." She throws the cushion back at me, but I catch it and place it back on the sofa.

When the TV screen comes to life, I sit up, straightening my spine. Bourbon News is at the airport with a load of other reporters. Hairs prickle on the back of my neck, wondering what's going on.

Then I see her.

Eve.

Twenty-Nine

EVE

Arriving at the airport, I turn to Jay. "What's going on? You'd think royalty were flying in with the crowd of local press at the airport." Maybe they are. I've been so wrapped up in my own issues. I haven't a clue what's happening in the world anymore.

Jolene, a reporter from BCN, waves me over.

"Who's flying in? Santa?" I giggle.

"We're here for you, silly."

"Me? I'm going home for the holidays."

"Have you checked your socials lately?"

Me? Checked my socials? I don't even have any. Other than the one post I made last night. My mouth forms an O. I pull my phone from my bag and go to the video app.

Ping. Ping. Ping. Ping.

The little red box at the bottom of my screen flashes up with hearts, speech bubbles, and a silhouette. I tap on my video to see 1.9 million views. My jaw drops.

Jay snatches the phone from my hand. "Cover me in eggnog and roll me in glitter."

"You've gone viral, Eve. How do you feel?" Jolene thrusts the mic in my face, and I realise all the cameras are on me. At least I look better today than I did on the video. I'd had too many red wines. Paired with my emotions, I wasn't thinking clearly.

"I just hope Liam sees it and gets in touch. I need him to know I'm in love with him, and I'm sorry for what I said."

"Are you the reason he's not doing any more unwrapped photographs?" A voice shouts from behind a barrier, held back by airport security.

"I don't know about that." Please let it be me. I close my eyes and say a silent Christmas wish.

Everyone fires off questions with each flash of their camera. They all jumble into one as I walk through the press. Jay wraps an arm around me in full protection mode as he pulls my case along. My legs shake with each step, unsure whether to check in now and wait for him in the departure lounge or wait here.

"I'll wait with you here if you like." Jay gives me a reassuring squeeze as we approach the doors to the terminal.

Once inside and away from the paparazzi, I sit near a large Christmas tree. Sprigs of mistletoe hang from a display, reminding me of our first kiss. I pull out my phone and scroll through the hundreds of messages on my video, hoping one will be from him. I'm not entirely sure how this app works, but he must have seen it, unless he hasn't been on the app.

His account has no new videos. My heart sinks. "Shall I go outside and give a statement? I could make the lunchtime news."

"It's worth a shot if you think he hasn't seen your video."

With a heavy heart and legs like lead weights, I step outside. Snowflakes glitter as they flutter down from the heavens. Noise erupts again, bringing my focus back to earth. Public speaking is something I should be used to. I do it every day in front of thousands, but I'm in front of a camera, not a live audience. "I'm not sure if Liam saw my video. Can anyone put out an appeal?"

They all shout at once. My heart is ready to burst with emotion that everyone's here for me, for us.

Jolene shouts, "I'll get you on." She thrusts the mic in my hand. "Go." She clicks her fingers to the cameraman.

"I'm here at terminal five." I wave my hand behind me. "I'm not sure if you saw my pathetic apology last night on that video app you love so much, but I'll say it again." The mic trembles in my hand, and I hold my jacket closed to block out the chill. "I'm sorry. I should have listened. Come back to me. Let me make it up to you and be your Christmas Eve. I'll be waiting inside, under the mistletoe."

Sitting on the bench next to the Christmas display, I see my appeal on the lunchtime news. I cringe, never able to watch myself on TV. Waiting for him, I scroll through all his different socials, looking for any sign of life. Nothing. It's like he's gone from posting three times a day to a total ban.

This is just my luck that he takes a social media break

when I need him. "Do you think he's seen the video and still isn't interested?"

"If that's the case, then he wasn't worth it in the first place." Jay hands me a chocolate bar he bought from the vending machine, but the jet stream in my stomach is making me nauseous.

An hour goes by and the loudspeaker calls the final check in for transatlantic flights. "I guess I best check in. Looks like he's not coming." I drag my case to the desk and hand over my ticket and passport. The local news plays on the TV, and his face pops up. I can't hear what he's saying as the TV is on mute, but he's in a car driving. Then it cuts to the reporter. "What was he saying?"

A blizzard billows in my stomach as I make my way back to the bench to check my phone. He's posted a new video. A roar erupts from the crowd outside, and I stand with my eyes fixed on the double glass doors.

He bursts through, carrying a bag on his back like Santa holding his sack. The press follow, hot on his heels. A smile spreads on his face when our eyes meet. He jogs over to me, shaking the dusting of snow from his dark hair, then drops his bag as he reaches the mistletoe. "Hey, frosty."

Happy tears leak from my eyes as I throw my arms around him, saturating him with love. "What took you so long?"

"I didn't see your video until the lunchtime news, then I had to drive back from Reagan Springs and get my passport from the apartment."

"Do you forgive me?" I blink away the tears as I gaze into his twinkling eyes, matching my own.

"Can you forgive me?" His hands slide around my back, holding me in a tight embrace.

With a sniffle, I say, "There's nothing to forgive. I should've listened and been more understanding."

His thumb swipes the tears from my cheek. "And I should have been more open from the beginning."

"We both need to work on our commination skills, I guess." A smile spreads across my face, knowing that when I get him alone, talking is the last thing I want to do with this man.

His smile mirrors my own as if he's thinking the same thing. "Talking of communication, what was that thing you said on your drunken video? I want to hear it again."

"I am sorry?"

"The other three little words." He quirks a grin, dipping his head slightly towards mine.

My heart swells as I realise the three words he's referring to. "I love you."

His lips press hard against my mouth, taking possession of me in a lightning kiss that forks out, sending a tingling electric current throughout my body.

"Eve, I love you, too. I've always loved you and your tormenting little pussy."

I burst into a fit of giggles.

Jay turns to the crowd and states, "For the record, he means her ginger cat."

The crowd erupts in laughter.

"Where's Diesel?"

"My sister has him."

"Liam, is Eve the reason you're stopping your unwrapped newsletters?" a voice shouts out.

I face the crowd, dazzled by the constant flashes.

"Yeah," Liam shouts over his shoulder, then cups my cheeks, kissing my nose. "From now on, I'm only unwrapped for you."

A lump chokes my throat, rendering me speechless for the first time ever. I love this man with all my heart.

Another voice shouts, "Does this mean you won't be donating to the cause any more?"

With his arm around me, he faces the crowd. "I still want to continue with my newsletters, if that's okay with the boss." He nods towards me with a grin. "Only the pictures won't be as intimate."

"But they'll still be hot," I say. "And knowing it's for a good cause, hopefully his fans won't be deterred."

The loudspeaker sounds, bringing us both down from cloud nine.

Liam takes my hand and lifts his bag from the floor. "Merry Christmas, everyone. We have a plane to catch."

I say my goodbyes to Jay who waves us off, and Liam waves to the press. Such a natural at all this. We dash through security and board the plane with little time to spare.

My shoulders relax into the seat. "I didn't think you were coming."

"I wasn't about to miss my Christmas Eve gift."

My eyes widen. "I don't have a Christmas gift for you."

Liam takes my hand, stroking his thumb over my skin. "You're my gift."

I smile, still feeling bad that I never bought him anything. "You still have the shirt, right?"

He chuckles. "Yeah."

"I promise I'll make it up to you. Maybe I can find a Yorkshire pudding recipe book when we land." My face beams at him, making my cheeks ache, but I can't stop smiling. "And I won't fight with you like cats and dogs."

He nuzzles into my neck. "Now I am disappointed."

A giggle escapes as I buckle up, grateful I don't need to ask for an extendable belt as I do on other flights.

"I hope your family likes me." Liam taps his foot and scratches his unshaven jaw.

I place my hand on his leg to settle his constant foot tapping. "They're gonna love you as much as I do."

The vulnerable look drops from his face as his lips curl into a smile brighter than a Christmas star, so full of pride and hope.

My heart soars, flying in the stratosphere as I gaze into his twinkling eyes. After so many single Christmases, Santa really has delivered this year.

Epilogue

LIAM

The music plays and everyone stands and turns to face the white double doors at the back of the room. I adjust my tie and straighten the lapel of my jacket, taking in a deep breath as I wait for my girl to walk down the aisle.

Graham stands at the altar, a nervous twitch underneath his grizzly beard. Eve's mom stands to my right and gives my arm a gentle squeeze of excitement as we all wait patiently for the doors to open. I tap my slacks pocket, checking I still have the small box and relax, letting out a long breath.

The doors open. A smile spans the breadth of my face when I see her—a vision in pink. The tiara adorning her hair twinkles under the lights of the room as she saunters down the aisle between tall vases filled to the brim with fresh flowers. Her smile pushes up her rosy cheeks when she glances at me through her thick lashes. My chest swells with pride, knowing she's my girl. Bourbon's most loved weather girl and the cleverest, kindest, and sexiest woman I know. It's been just over a year since we met that day in the park and living with her since Christmas has been the best year of my life.

The crowd coos as Jay walks behind her all done up in a white glittering shirt, holding his momma's arm with tears in his eyes, but I can't stop beaming at my girl. She sits in the aisle seat next to me, and I give her a kiss on her cheek.

"You look beautiful."

She holds my hand, interlacing our fingers. "You don't look so bad yourself."

Jay kisses his mom and stands in front of Graham, both of them dopey-eyed. Even Graham, who's usually this big grizzly bear, has turned into a cuddly teddy. It's about time they tied the knot. Ever since Jay started coming round to Graham's place when he lived next door, I could tell they were made for each other. Opposites attract after all. Look at Eve and I. We bring out the best in each other and balance each other perfectly.

She's really jumped on board with my charity work. Being a private person with no social media, it's nice when she allows me to send out a picture of us both together, just a casual picture of us in the park with Diesel or both of us at our favourite Mexican restaurant. My fans really lap that up, making me so happy that they not only accept her, but have fallen in love with her as I have.

"We are gathered here today..." the preacher begins her speech and I shuffle in the seat, getting comfy, knowing how these things can drag on.

I glance at Eve, her eyes tearing up. We've had a busy

year setting up my own gym, "All Bodies Are Good Bodies." Eve helped me pick the name. We get people of all shapes and sizes who just want to work out to be fit and healthy and not just keep up appearances, as she says.

Eve's mom hands me a tissue, nodding towards Eve, and I dab under her eyes. She takes it from me, clutching it between her palms on top of the layers of pink tulle covering her legs. Trust Jay to pick out the frilliest and most glitzy dress he could find. I smile to myself. She looks like a sparkly fairy atop a Christmas tree. All she needs is a fairy wand. Perhaps after tonight, she will make all my wishes come true.

The happy couple kiss and then sign the register before walking out of the ceremony hand in hand to Kenny Rogers' and Dolly Parton's "Islands in the Stream."

I take Eve's hand and the crowd follows outside for the photographs. Graham and Jay have spared no expense on this wedding. The hotel is the most prestigious in Bourbon, and I cannot wait to make use of the four-poster bed tonight.

EVE

Watching Uncle Graham and Jay finally say "I do" gives me a warm and fuzzy feeling inside. The wedding ceremony was beautiful. A little lavish for me, but it fitted them perfectly. "Nothing's Gonna Stop Us Now" by Starship plays as they take to the dance floor for their first dance. Jay's white sequinned shirt glitters under the disco lights, making me smile as he spins Graham around the floor.

Graham laughs and allows Jay his moment before taking the dominant role and holding him close into more of a slow sway, which Graham seems more comfortable with. My heart swells again.

I've always loved weddings, but they're even more special when it's someone you love dearly and you're able to be part of their day.

The song blends into "It's Raining Men" and a flurry of their friends jump to their feet.

Liam's body jiggles at the side of me. "Wanna dance?" His foot taps uncontrollably, causing the tulle on my skirt to shake. Something he usually does when he's nervous, but I'm wondering if he just likes this song?

"I didn't know you liked The Weather Girls." I cock an eyebrow his way.

He chuckles. "I can still surprise you, frosty." He stands from the frilly chair covered in a big pink organza bow, and pulls me to my feet. A giggle bursts from my lips watching him shake his arse as we walk to the square tiled floor dazzling with multicoloured disco lights. He's never been shy; his confidence made me fall in love with him.

Liam spins me around, my long, layered tulle skirt fanning out, making me feel like a prom queen, especially the way Liam's looking at me. He interlaces our fingers, singing along to the song, and lifts our arms above our heads. His rough hands roam my body, moving over the pink sequinned bodice, then he bends, planting kisses down my chest, before coming back to my face.

I throw my arms around his neck as the song changes

and follow his movements as he rocks into me. The smile on his face reaches his eyes, causing a flutter in my chest. He pulls me closer, still swaying his hips and singing along to the lyrics of Erasure's "A Little Respect." I mime the lyrics, telling him, "I'm so in love with you."

He smothers my mouth, his tongue delves between my parted lips and after a year of being together, each kiss with him still has my heart racing like it's the first time. The lights around us turn into a kaleidoscope of colour, as if I'm high from his kiss like a psychedelic drug. I hum against his mouth and he deepens the kiss, licking every corner of my mouth as if dying of thirst.

The song is forgotten, along with the crowd, as he makes out with me on the dance floor. His body stills, but I feel him harden even through the mass of tulle. He breaks the kiss, cupping my face and pulling away slightly to gaze into my eyes, his full of want and need.

"Come on." With urgency, he grips my wrist, dragging me towards the exit. Once outside of the hotel's reception area, we rush through the gardens lit up by twinkling fairy lights and Christmas candy canes.

"Where are we going? It's freezing out here." But despite the icy chill, the magical winter wonderland lights up my insides, reminding me of my patio that he decked out for me last year. We arrive at a small pavilion in the centre decorated with flowers and lights. The scene surrounding his magnificent face is truly spectacular.

"Did you know this was here?" I hold on to his hands while taking in the round gazebo stone structure with arched windows.

"Yeah, I had a look around earlier while you were

getting dressed." Liam takes off his jacket, placing it over my shoulders. The soft music drifts in from the distance, and I warm up instantly as his fingers graze from my cheek to my neck and over my chest. "Do you know how fucking perfect you are, Eve?"

I swallow. My teenage self would never believe I would be this happy with a man, but here I am, pinching myself yet again. "Yes, you tell me almost every day." A giggle escapes and I peck his lips, but he fists my curls, holding my head in place.

"I don't think you know just how much I love you." His voice trembles like he's straining.

"I know, Liam."

"I don't think you do. I think I need to show you." He drops to his knees, and I check our surroundings. A smile pushes my cheeks up when I realise we're hidden behind the stone wall of the pavilion, knowing he's about to bury his face between my thighs, just like he did this morning.

The anticipation bubbles in my veins and my core clenches. He gazes up at me from his one-knee position on the cold slab floor with a smirk on his face.

I pinch my eyebrows together. "What is it?"

He pulls a small box from his pocket. My breath halts. He opens the box to reveal a cluster of diamonds in the shape of a snowflake attached to a platinum band. The fairy lights hanging from above make it shine brighter than the Christmas star in the heavens, and my heart soars once again, taking flight through the galaxy like a supernova.

"Marry me, frosty. Marry me and make me the happiest man alive."

My words won't come out past the bauble lodged in my throat. Instead, I nod, causing a tear to drip onto my cheek.

He slides the diamond onto my ring finger and shoves the box back in his pocket. "Right, let me see if I can dissolve those tears and put a smile back on that pretty face of yours." Ruffling through the layers of tulle, he finds my bare legs, wrapping his rough hands around my ankles before gliding over my calves to squeeze my chunky thighs.

Liam disappears under my frilled skirt, and I gasp as his hot breath finds my sensitive spot. With his teasing fingers, he tugs at the satin underwear, letting it pool at my feet. "Wider, Eve." His nose nudges between my folds. I lean back against the stone wall and widen my stance.

A shudder courses through me as his tongue pierces my entrance, prodding through the wall of muscle, and I moan out his name. Teeth graze my folds, quickly replaced by his tongue as he laps me up, licking my bundle of nerves with perfect rhythm and precision. He knows exactly what I like and how to make me come over and over again.

Footsteps click against the pavement. I freeze. Liam continues licking me out, devouring me like a Christmas trifle, clearly all sounds muffled by my thick thighs against his ears like a pair of warm earmuffs. My fingers curl into the fabric of my dress and bunch the tulle in my fists to stop my body jerking with pleasure.

"Eve, I wondered where you got to. Your mother's looking for you." Jay brings a cigarette to his lips and sucks in as he flicks his lighter. The cherry glows red, much like my face, not to mention my clit throbbing with heat as Liam continues to lick at my core.

Not now. Not my mother. My eyes widen, staring at the

cigarette, hoping Jay doesn't glance down, but I can't shift the delirious smile on my face.

"Where's Liam disappeared to?" He exhales the smoke, watching it swirl into the cool night air.

Liam stills. Probably aware we have company. I feel him shuffle farther between my legs like Diesel or Jingles trying to hide when they're being naughty.

I can't speak, and cover my hand under the layers of tulle. The last thing I need is Jay seeing my engagement ring and coming over to congratulate me with a hug and tripping over the man at my feet buried beneath my skirt.

Jay takes another long drag. "Are you okay, Eve?"

"I...er...I."

Jay's gaze floats down my dress. His pupils dilate. I look down to find the sole of Liam's shoe poking out from under the tulle. My face heats, glowing as red as Jay's cigarette.

"Liam gone downtown, has he?" He chuckles, taking another inhale. "Don't worry, Eve. I'll keep your mother busy." He stubs out his cigarette against the stone wall and walks down the two steps of the pavilion with a chuckle. "I'll keep your secret as long you don't tell Graham I was having a cheeky smoke."

I give him a sheepish smile.

He pops a piece of gum into his mouth. "How long do you need?"

"Er... five minutes." I wring the tulle around my hands nervously, knowing once Jay's gone, I'm about to detonate over Liam's face.

"Half an hour," Liam shouts, his voice muffled by my legs and the fabric.

Jay waves a hand and rushes down the path, telling another couple that the pavilion is off limits. I sag against the wall. The tension from my body relaxes as Liam kisses between my thighs.

He lifts his head from under my skirt. "Has he gone?"

I nod, biting my lip, but missing the feel of his warm breath on my legs.

"Damn, it's hot under there." His lips crash to mine, his fingers make quick work of undoing his belt and springing free his erection. Rough hands hike up the layers to my dress until his palms hold my behind and hoist me up into his arms. I wrap my legs around him, leaving my satin knickers hanging from one foot stuck to my shoe.

He sinks into my wet heat, pinning me against the wall, holding me up with his bulging biceps. "I can't wait to make you Mrs. Walker."

I moan against his lips, my arms clinging to his shoulders as he ruts into me with deep, punishing thrusts. "Mrs. Snow-Walker."

He flinches his head back. "Snow-Walker?"

"Yes, I like my name." My fists knot in his shirt, his engorged length catching the perfect spot from this angle each time he thrusts into me.

He bites down on my neck, sending a shockwave of pleasure straight to my centre. "Mrs. Walker-Snow."

"Whatever you say." I can't think straight or argue when he has me like this. "Fuck me harder, Liam, make me come."

"You asked for it." Both hands squeeze my ass as he buries himself deep, pulling out and plunging back in at only a pace he can sustain.

The tulle between us wafts in our face between each bruising thrust, and I roll my head back. With my fingers clenched, thighs dripping, legs shaking, I see stars.

"That's it, frosty." He covers my lips before I cry out my orgasm, then he grunts into my mouth with his own release. "I'll never get bored seeing your nose crinkle like that." His lips delicately press against my nose, then shower me with kisses around my face.

"I love you, Liam."

"I love you, Eve. So fucking much." He slips out of me and steps back, lowering my legs. My heels click on the ground, and he bends down to untangle my satin knickers from the strap on my shoe.

Warm cum slips down between my thighs, causing another wave of tingles to course through my bloodstream. "I need to clean up."

Liam checks his pockets. "I don't have any tissue." He fingers his tie. "I don't think I need this now, do I?" Unravelling it from the knot around his neck, he then folds it between his fingers and uses it to swipe between my thighs. He folds it again and swipes once more before tucking it into his trouser pocket.

I pull up my knickers, then straighten my skirt. Liam hovers above me with a smile on his face. The chilly air no longer bothers me after our little workout, and his smile always stokes the fire in me.

My hand smoothes over his shirt and the light catches in my snowflake diamond ring, causing my heart to overflow with pure happiness. "I think we should keep this between us tonight."

"Well, I wasn't gonna tell anyone, frosty. I doubt the guests want to know about our warm-up."

I swat his chest. "I mean our engagement."

A smile spans the width of his face. "Oh yeah, that. You know I can keep a secret, but not for long. Tonight is Jay and Graham's night, but after that, I want the whole world to know you're mine."

He takes my hand in his and kisses my knuckles as we walk down the steps of the pavilion. He pulls out his phone and starts snapping photographs. I hold up my hand, showing off the ring, and he presses the record button as he holds my fingers and says into the camera, "She said yes." His lips press against mine as he holds the camera in front of us, recording this magical moment. The goofy grin on Liam's face makes me giggle as he pulls away to stop the recording.

"I have a feeling that's gonna be doing the rounds on your socials tomorrow?" I give him an eye roll, but secretly love how he wants to show me off all the time.

"Our fans can share this moment with us, but not our wedding. I want our wedding to be a small, private family affair."

I squish my eyebrows together in pure surprise. "Really? Not even a photograph?"

He shrugs a shoulder. "Well, maybe just one photo to the highest bidding magazine."

I know what he's thinking. Any money we make from such publicity goes towards his charity, and I couldn't think of a better way to raise funds than selling a picture of us celebrating our love for each other.

He pulls me close, dropping his arm over my shoulder. "Just promise me one thing, though."

"Anything."

"Don't take Jay with you to pick out your wedding dress."

A burst of laughter leaves our lips. I lean into him, inhaling the scent of my arousal on his face, then kiss his jaw as we walk back to the party, ready to live the rest of my life with this man. To have and to hold from this day forward, for better, for worse, for richer, for poorer, in sickness and in health, to love and to cherish, until death do us part.

Enjoyed the book?

Your opinion matters, and reviews make an author's world go round!

Please leave me a review on
Amazon, Goodreads & Bookbub.

Thanks for reading!
Annie

Looking for more books like this?
Check out **Hate Tea Love You**
A Man of The Month Club Novella

Curves for Christmas

Single Dad Santa by Heather Lauren
One Night With Santa By Eve London
The Christmas Seduction by Robecca Austin
Snow One Like You by Haven Rose
Caught Red Handed by Melverna McFarlane
His Christmas Obsession by Sadie King
Sugar Plum Daddy by Rebecca Gallo
Sugar Cookie Kisses by Aubree Valentine
Secret Santa by Willow Sanders
Snow Thanks by Layne Daniels
Frost My Cookie by J Preston
My Holiday Surprise by Jessa Joy
Tangled in Tinsel by Kamaria Sweet
Under the Mistletoe by Sammi Starlight
Christmas Star by Lana Love
Blissful Vixen by Jade Royal
Unwrapped for You by Annie Charme
Second Chance Scrooge by JJ Grice
His Fake Holidate by Anne Lange
The Daddy Clause by Josie O'Sullivan
Owned for Xmas by Imani Jay

Acknowledgments

Firstly I want to thank all my readers. Writing a book takes so much of my time and sanity, but with each like, comment, review, or message, it makes everything worth while. I want to continue to write real characters that we can all relate to and it's your continued support that spurs me on.

My family and friends, thank you for all your support.

My pets for the inspiration.

To my critique partners, JL Reed, Jo, Kat, Jenni, Amy, Amie, Larissa and Elin. Thank you so much for your input on this book, as well as your continued support and friendship.

For my ARC readers. I appreciate each and every one of you for taking the time to review my work. Thank you.

And last but not least, the amazingly talented authors in the Curves for Christmas collaboration, it's been a pleasure working with you all and I look forward to doing again. Your professionalism and support has made this collaboration work like a dream. Thank you.

Also by Annie Charme

Spicy RomCom

Hate Tea Love You

A Man of The Month Club Novella

Tease The Season

A Man of The Month Club Christmas in July Novella

Kiss and Shell

A Man of The Month Club Novella

Kissmas Reunion

A Man of The Month Club Novella

When My Ship Comes In

A Naughty Nautical Romance

Twisted Santa

A Sweet but Twisted Novella

Unwrapped For You

A Curves For Christmas Novella

Snowed in with the Dad Bod

A Dad Bod Christmas Novella

❄

The Temptation Series

Forever Young

A Prequel, The Temptation Series

Forever Yours

Book 1 of The Temptation Series

Forever Mine

Book 2 of The Temptation Series

The Sinful Secrets Series

A little darker themed (cosy dark romance)

Protecting Poppy

Age Gap Curvy Girl Romance with Suspense

Taming Violet

Age Gap Curvy Girl Mystery Romance

Pursuing Lilly

Age Gap Curvy Girl Off-Limits Romance

About the Author

Annie Charme lives in the heart of England with her husband, two children and a randy dog.
She is a graphic artist by day and author by night.
When she isn't working, you will find her enjoying time with her family in the English countryside or curled up on the sofa with a coffee, blanket, dog and a steamy book.

Being an avid reader of romance novels, Annie feels that the larger woman is not represented enough, and books about plus size women are very few and far between. This is something that sparked her passion for writing.

www.anniecharme.com